Enchanted Palace

ISBN 978-0545-66769-2

Text copyright © 2012 by Hothouse Fiction Limited.
Illustrations copyright © 2012 by Orchard Books.

All rights reserved. Published by Scholastic Inc., 557 Broadway, New York, NY 10012 by arrangement with Orchard Books. SCHOLASTIC and associated logos are trademarks and/or registered trademarks of Scholastic Inc.

12 11 10 9 8 7 6 5 4 3 2 1   14 15 16 17 18 19/0

Printed in the U.S.A.   40
This edition first printing, January 2014

Enchanted Palace

ROSIE BANKS

Scholastic Inc.

Contents

A Mysterious Find

"I think I'm finished now, ma'am. Where would you like this box to go?" Summer Hammond asked as she packed up the last two books from her station.

"I'm finished here, too," Jasmine Smith added, putting the last things into a box.

Mrs. Benson smiled. "Goodness! That was fast work, girls. Well done."

Ellie Macdonald poked her head up from behind a table, tucking a wiry red curl behind her ear. "Hey, nobody told me it was a race!" Laughter danced in her green eyes as she stood up.

Jasmine winked at Summer. "It looks like we're the champions!"

"You're all champions," Mrs. Benson said as she smiled at the three girls. "This was the school's most successful rummage sale ever, and it was all thanks to you!"

Although they were all very different from one another, Ellie, Summer, and Jasmine were as close as sisters. They all

lived in the same town and had been best friends since they first started elementary school.

Summer was shy, and tugged at her blond braids whenever she felt nervous. She often had her head buried in a book, either reading about the natural world or writing poems and stories about her animal friends.

Jasmine was outgoing and always in a hurry, with her long dark hair whipping around her as she raced from one thing to another. She loved singing and dancing and being in the spotlight.

Ellie was a joker, and was always the first to laugh at her own clumsiness. She was also very artistic and loved drawing. Together the girls made quite a team!

"It was nothing really," Summer said, blushing at their teacher's praise. "The books I sold were mostly my old ones from our attic."

"Well, they were very popular," said Mrs. Benson. "And, Jasmine, you played that guitar wonderfully. After everyone heard you, we sold it in no time."

Jasmine grinned. "No problem, Mrs. Benson. You know I love music!"

"And the fashion boutique was a great success, too — especially those superb Ellie Macdonald designs!" Mrs. Benson picked up a T-shirt with a bold green-and-purple pattern on it. She looked over at Ellie. "Thanks so much for making one for me."

"Do you like the design?" Ellie said. "Green and purple are my favorite colors."

"You don't say!" Jasmine's hazel eyes

twinkled with amusement as she looked at her friend's flowery purple-and-green dress, her green leggings, and her purple ballet flats!

Ellie chuckled, then turned to pick up her bag. But as she did, she tripped over something and fell to the floor with a *thump*.

"Ouch!"

"Are you okay?" asked Mrs. Benson.

"I'm fine — it's just my two left feet, as usual!" Ellie said as she stood up. "But what's this?"

She picked up the object she'd tripped over — an old wooden box. It was as large as her outstretched hand and made out of solid wood with a curved lid. The whole thing was thick with dust, but under the grime Ellie could tell the box was beautiful. Its sides were carved with intricate patterns that she couldn't quite make out, and on the lid was a mirror, surrounded by six glass stones. Ellie wiped the lid with her sleeve and could just see her reflection. As she held the box, light swirled in the stones. It looked almost . . . magical. "How strange," she murmured. "I'm sure it wasn't here a minute ago."

Jasmine took the box and tried to open it. "The lid's stuck down," she said. "It won't budge."

Mrs. Benson glanced at her watch. "Well, wherever it came from, it's too late to sell it now. Why don't you girls take it home — you never know, you might find a way to open it."

"Ooh, yes please!" Summer breathed. "It's really pretty. We could use it to put jewelry in. Let's take it to my house and try to get it open. I live the closest!"

The girls waved good-bye to Mrs. Benson and raced out of the school playground. They all lived in a small town called Honeyvale, which was surrounded by hills and beautiful countryside. Summer's house was only a few minutes away from the school, just past the post office and Mrs. Mill's sweet shop. Mrs. Mill waved as the girls flew by — she was used to seeing Summer, Ellie, and Jasmine together!

When they arrived at her house, Summer eagerly opened her front door and they pounded up the stairs, calling out a quick hello to Mrs. Hammond before spilling into Summer's bedroom.

The walls were covered in wildlife posters, and books were stacked neatly on their shelves. Summer dropped down onto her white fluffy rug. Jasmine and Ellie joined her, placing the carved wooden box in front of them. Summer's cat, Rosa, came over and sniffed at it with interest.

"What do we do now?" Ellie asked.

Jasmine grabbed a box of tissues from Summer's bedside table. "We clean it."

The three friends worked together, wiping away the dust and dirt that covered the box.

"Wow. It's absolutely gorgeous!" exclaimed Summer. She traced her finger over the side of the box. Now that it was clean, she could see that the sides were covered in delicate carvings of fairies, unicorns, and other magical creatures.

The glass stones that studded the lid were a deep green, and shone like emeralds.

"What do you think is inside?" Ellie whispered.

Jasmine shrugged. "Let's try opening it again."

Ellie passed Jasmine a ruler from Summer's desk and they carefully tried to pry the lid open, but it refused to budge.

Summer sighed. "There has to be a way to open it." She rubbed at the mirrored glass of the lid with a tissue to clean away the last traces of dust, then gasped. "The mirror. It's . . . glowing!"

"It is," squeaked Ellie, staring wide-eyed at the box. "And look — there are words in it!"

Jasmine frowned. With a shaky voice she read out the words that had appeared:

"Ten digits make two,
Though two are too few.
But three lots of two,
On each jewel will do."

The three friends looked at one another in amazement.

"Is–is it a trick?" Summer stammered.

"Or maybe magic?" Ellie whispered.

"I don't know," Jasmine said thoughtfully. "But the words look like a riddle. My grandmother is always giving me Hindi riddles to solve. She says it's good for my brain."

"Do you think you can solve this one?" Ellie asked.

Jasmine stared at the words. "Well," she began, "Grandma says that riddles don't always mean what they seem to mean. You've got to look at things sideways. 'Ten digits make two . . .' Well, the word *digits* normally means 'numbers,' but it can also mean 'fingers,' right?"

Summer and Ellie nodded.

Jasmine sat up a bit straighter. "So if 'ten digits' refers to your fingers and thumbs, that would make two . . ."

"Hands!" Ellie finished. "Ten digits make two hands! 'Though two are too few,' so two hands aren't enough!"

"'But three lots of two, on each jewel will do,'" said Summer. "So 'three lots of two' means three sets of hands."

Ellie's eyes gleamed. "That's it! The riddle is telling the three of us to put our hands on the green jewels!"

"What are we waiting for?" Jasmine said. "Let's do it!" She placed her hands on two of the glinting stones. Ellie and Summer hesitated for a moment but then lowered their palms to the jewels, too.

Their hands completely covered the box.

It might just have been Jasmine's and
Ellie's hands next to hers, but it seemed
to Summer that the box was growing
warmer underneath her touch. "Can
you feel that?" she whispered. Ellie and
Jasmine nodded, their eyes wide with
amazement.

Suddenly, the mirror glowed brightly
and light spilled out from between
their fingers. Gasping, the girls moved their
hands — and the box burst open! A beam
of glittering light streamed out and
bounced off the walls of Summer's
bedroom. The girls watched in awe as the
beam hit her wardrobe, and disappeared.

"Wow! Did you see that?" Ellie cried,
staring down at the box, which was shut

again as if nothing had happened. The others nodded. "I wonder if —"

Suddenly, she was interrupted by hangers clattering inside Summer's wardrobe.

"It's dark, so dark," wailed a deep voice.

"Please calm down, Your Majesty," a girl's tinkly voice replied. "I'll find a way out."

"Ouch!" cried the other voice. "Careful where you put your elbows, Trixibelle!"

Summer, Ellie, and Jasmine stared at one another in astonishment.

"Does your wardrobe normally do that?" Ellie asked Summer.

"Um, no. M-m-maybe we should hide?" Summer looked pale.

Just then, the wardrobe door wobbled, and all three girls leapt to their feet.

"Ah, here it is. I think I've found a way out," the tinkly voice said.

Jasmine narrowed her eyes. She grabbed Summer's ruler and held it out in front of her like a sword.

"Who's there?" she shouted bravely.

As if in answer, the wardrobe door sprang open and something small and colorful zoomed out into the air. Sparks flew everywhere as it whirled around the room. Then, silently and delicately, a tiny girl came to a stop above Summer's bedside table. A girl floating on a leaf!

Unexpected Visitors

The tiny person was hardly bigger than Summer's pencil case, but she was the most gorgeous creature that the girls had ever seen. Her messy blond hair peeked out from under a flower hat, which matched her colorful dress, pretty bracelets, and shiny ring. She had big, bright blue eyes, cute pointy ears, and a dazzling smile.

"She can't be real," Jasmine murmured, staring in wonder.

"Do you think she's a-a-a . . ." Summer could barely finish her sentence.

"A pixie?" The pretty creature smiled. "Yes! And of course I'm real," she said, doing a loop-the-loop on her leaf. "I'm Trixibelle — Trixi, for short — and I'm a royal pixie. And who are you?"

Ellie and Summer were too surprised to speak. There was an actual pixie in front of them! Finally, Jasmine, who was always the boldest, stepped forward and introduced herself.

"I'm Jasmine. And this is Ellie and Summer." She pointed at her friends.

"Summer, Jasmine, and Ellie," Trixi repeated. Suddenly the large, shiny ring on her finger twinkled with magic. She tapped it and a burst of sparkles shot out, forming their names in glittery writing in the air. "What lovely names!"

The three friends gasped in delight as the sparkles floated down and landed on their skin like snowflakes.

"Trixi! Where have you gone?" a voice yelped from inside the wardrobe. There was a *crash* and a pile of clothes tumbled out the door. A

small, rosy-cheeked man, the same height as Jasmine, emerged from under the clothes. He was dressed in a purple velvet robe trimmed with white feathers, and he wore half-moon spectacles perched on the end of his nose. He had a pointy beard, and a gleaming crown sat at a jaunty angle on his thick, curly, white hair.

Trixi gave a little curtsy. "May I present King Merry, ruler of the Secret Kingdom," she said, zooming over to him on her leaf and pulling a yellow sock off one of the points of his crown.

The girls looked at one another, then quickly curtsied as well.

"Pleased to meet you," Jasmine said in her most polite voice. "But what are you doing in Summer's bedroom?"

"And what on earth is the Secret Kingdom?" Ellie added, finally finding her voice.

The king adjusted his spectacles and peered at the girls. But instead of answering their questions, he said, "Oh my. Are you humans? Trixi, what's going on?"

"I believe we are in the Other Realm, Sire," Trixi said, her face shining with excitement.

"Goodness me!" said King Merry. "No one from our kingdom has visited the Other Realm for a very long time." He stared at the girls. "You see, the Secret Kingdom and your world, which we call the Other Realm, exist side by side but our paths rarely cross. I don't know how we've come to be here."

Trixi looked around the room and spotted the carved box on the rug. "Look! There's your Magic Box, Your Majesty. Its power must have brought us here."

"This box belongs to you?" Summer asked, looking confused.

"Yes, it does," the king said with a pleased smile.

"And what sort of Magic Box is it?" said Jasmine, looking at it.

"It's one of my inventions!" King Merry said proudly. "I'm not exactly sure what it does yet, though." He sighed. "I invented it because I need something to show me a way to save my kingdom from Queen Malice's meanness. The next thing I knew, the box had disappeared, and we were in your wardrobe!"

"Wait a minute," Ellie said. "Who's Queen Malice?"

"She's my sister." King Merry took off his crown and anxiously rubbed at his forehead. "You see, my home is a place of great beauty. A place where unicorns graze in emerald fields and mermaids live in aquamarine seas. But my sister, Malice, can't bear to see that beauty. She wants to make everything as dull and dreary as she is, and take all happiness from the land." King Merry stopped, his eyes welling up.

Trixi quickly tapped her ring and a white hanky appeared. King Merry blew his nose noisily before continuing.

"Ever since the people of the Secret Kingdom chose me as their ruler instead of her, she has tried to get revenge on us all by using her magic to make everyone miserable."

Trixi folded her arms angrily. "And now, on King Merry's thousandth birthday, Queen Malice has done the worst thing ever! She's used her mean magic to make six horrible thunderbolts and fired them all into the kingdom. Each one carries a powerful spell designed to cause a terrible problem. But we don't know where they've landed or what trouble they will cause."

The king picked up the Magic Box and examined it closely. "I hoped this box could help me, but instead I've ended up in the Other Realm! It's baffling." He held the box out toward the girls. "You might as well keep it. It can't help me if its magic has gone all wonky."

Summer, Jasmine, and Ellie all leaned over to look at the box. Almost instantly a ripple of light spread across the box's lid, and another riddle appeared in the mirror! Ellie read it aloud:

"Look no further than your nose,
Look no further than your toes!
When you gaze at me you'll see,
The answer's clear as one, two, three!"

King Merry stamped his foot. "See! The box is all wonky! It's total nonsense!"

"It's a riddle, Your Majesty," Jasmine explained. "We've already solved one of them. I think we should try to solve this one — it could be a clue."

King Merry frowned. "All right. Well, since I invented the box, I suppose I should give it a try."

Jasmine nodded.

"Hmm . . . 'no further than your nose . . . no further than your toes . . .'" the king murmured.

The girls watched doubtfully as he crossed his eyes to look at his nose, then leaned forward to peer at his feet.

"Whoops!" The king's arms began to whirl like windmills as he tried to keep his balance. He fell onto the rug with a *bump.* "I told you it was nonsense," King Merry said sulkily, crossing his arms.

Jasmine, Summer, and Ellie looked down at the mysterious box again.

" 'When you gaze at me you'll see, the answer's clear as one, two, three!' " Ellie said. "That's it!"

"What's it?" asked King Merry, looking confused.

"I think the Magic Box is saying that the three of us can help you!" Ellie cried, pointing at the mirror's reflection of herself and her friends.

"Of course!" Trixi clapped her hands in delight. "The king's inventions never normally work this well!" she whispered in Ellie's ear.

"What was that, Trixi?" asked King Merry, raising his eyebrows.

Trixi tried to look innocent. "Nothing, Sire. I was just saying that your inventions always work in the end."

The king considered Trixi's words and then smiled. "Yes, yes, indeed they do!"

Then he peered at the girls over his spectacles. "The Secret Kingdom is in terrible trouble. Queen Malice will stop

at nothing to spread unhappiness. I rather think that you three girls may be our only hope! Will you help us?"

Ellie glanced eagerly at both of her friends. "We'll do anything we can!"

The Place You Love Most

"You try and stop us!" Jasmine cried.

Even Summer was excited, despite still being a bit uncertain. "Can we go now?" she asked. "I can't wait to meet all the magical creatures, and —"

She stopped as the mirror on the Magic Box started flashing again, and another riddle appeared. Summer read it out loud:

"The thunderbolt is hidden close,
In the place the king loves most.
Magic made to stop the fun,
Must be found before day's done."

Trixi frowned. "Well, King Merry loves
the Secret Kingdom more than anywhere
else, but it's so big. We'll never find the
thunderbolt."

"I think the riddle must mean
somewhere special," Jasmine said slowly.
"Where's your favorite place in the
Secret Kingdom, King Merry?"

"Oh, that's easy," the king replied. "It's
the Wandering Waterfalls." He scratched
his head. "Um, hang on . . . I do love the
Topaz Downs. And the Mystic Meadows
are wonderful during a pixie toadstool
fight." The king shook his head. "Oh dear,

I can't decide," he wailed. "There are so many places I love in the Secret Kingdom. I wish I was back in my palace, on my special snuggly throne. I always think best there."

"Maybe that's because you're happiest there," Ellie said, her eyes lighting up. "Perhaps your palace is the place you love most."

"Why, I think you're right!" the king exclaimed happily.

Trixi bit her lip anxiously. "But King Merry's birthday party is being held at the palace today! If the first thunderbolt is hidden there, Queen Malice's spell will ruin everything! We must leave for the Secret Kingdom right away."

Jasmine felt a buzz of excitement go through her. "How are we going to get there? Are we going to use magic?"

"Hang on, we can't just leave," Summer said, suddenly thinking of her mom and brothers, who were downstairs. "What do we tell our parents?"

"Don't worry," said Trixi. "My magic combined with the power of the Magic Box will easily transport you to the Secret Kingdom. And while the three of you are there, time will stand still in your world — nobody will even notice that you're gone."

Ellie's eyes sparkled. "Then what are we waiting for?"

She held out the Magic Box to Trixi, who tapped the lid with her ring and chanted:

"The evil queen has trouble planned.
Brave helpers fly to save our land!"

Trixi's words appeared on the mirrored lid and then soared toward the ceiling. Then the letters separated and descended like a cloud of sparkly butterflies. They began to whiz around the girls' heads until they formed a whirlwind.

"Place the Magic Box on the ground and hold one another's hands," Trixi called.

The whirlwind now filled the whole

room. Jasmine squeaked in delight as
she felt her feet leaving the ground. She
looked around and saw that Summer and
Ellie had also been picked up by the
magical storm. She squeezed their hands
encouragingly and her friends grinned

back. The king had his hands over his eyes, and Trixi was hovering just above his shoulder.

"Secret Kingdom, here we come!" Jasmine cried.

Then, in a flash of light, they were gone!

The Secret Kingdom

With a gentle bump, Jasmine landed on
something soft, white, and feathery.
"Wow!" she squealed. The girls were
each sitting on the back of a giant swan,
soaring through a bluebell-colored sky.

King Merry was riding another swan,
which was bigger than the others and
the tips of its wings sparkled with golden
feathers.

"Enjoying the ride?" Trixi asked Summer, as she zipped along next to them on her leaf.

Summer nodded enthusiastically. "Where did these swans come from?" she asked, staring at their snowy whiteness.

"They're King Merry's royal swans," Trixi replied. "They're taking us to his palace."

"They're so beautiful," Summer murmured, reaching out and stroking her swan's downy back.

"This is AMAZING!" Jasmine shouted as her swan took the lead, soaring through the clouds. "It's so much better than the SkyRyde at the Honeyvale Fair!"

"I'm not sure about that," Ellie wailed, her face pale as she clung on tightly to her swan. "At least the SkyRyde ends after three minutes."

"You're doing really well, Ellie," Summer called over encouragingly, knowing that her friend was afraid of heights. "But you should look if you can — it's so beautiful!"

Ellie peeked over her swan's broad wing and gasped. Beneath them was a beautiful island, shaped like a crescent moon and set in an aquamarine sea. The shore of the island glittered with golden sand, and in the distance the girls could see emerald-green hills and fields filled with little balls of light on golden stems.

"They must be *sun* flowers," Ellie said to herself, giggling. For a moment, she even forgot how high up they were!

As they descended through the fluffy white clouds, Jasmine felt her stomach flip-flop as she saw mermaids — real mermaids — sitting on shimmering rocks, combing their silvery hair. She could even hear their voices singing a hauntingly beautiful song.

"Welcome to the Secret Kingdom," Trixi said with a grin.

As they swooped down over the island, a fluttering flock of dragonflies rose up to meet them. A medley of colors surrounded them and Summer giggled in delight as one delicately landed on her hair.

"It's the most gorgeous hair clip ever!" Ellie laughed as she admired the dragonfly's beautiful, colorful wings.

King Merry proudly pointed out areas of the kingdom as they passed: the fairy flying school at the Windy Weir; Magic Mountain, filled with sparkling snow-covered slopes and ice slides; and Unicorn Valley, with its racecourse and enormous magical tree.

"Wow! Is that your palace, King Merry?" Jasmine asked, pointing to a fairytale castle nestled between two hills. A deep sapphire-blue moat hugged the castle walls, and magic seemed to glitter on the coral-pink bricks of the palace. The golden spires of the four palace turrets were studded with rubies and shone in the bright sunlight.

King Merry nodded. "Home, sweet home."

The swans landed safely in front of the palace gates and Ellie slipped gratefully to the ground, followed by Summer and Jasmine.

Trixi flew over to them. "Did you enjoy that, girls?"

"The kingdom is beautiful," Ellie said. "But I'm very happy to be on the ground again!"

"You must be joking, Ellie," Jasmine exclaimed with a grin. "I thought it was the best thing ever. I can't wait to ride on a swan again!"

"And it's just the beginning!" King Merry boomed. "Follow me."

He led them over to the gates. The golden railings twisted upward into the shape of a mighty oak. As the king pushed them open, the branches flowered and a fanfare sounded all around them.

"The king is here!" Trixi announced as they walked into the beautiful courtyard.

A group of friendly, green elf butlers, dressed in long black coats and white gloves, all turned and bowed. Then they returned to hanging streamers in the trees.

As the three girls looked closely, they saw that hundreds of glowing fireflies were clinging to the strings to make little lights.

"Oh my," the king breathed. "How handsome the twinkle-twinkle bunting looks. Trixi, my suggestion for the streamers has worked beautifully!"

"I never doubted that your idea would work, Sire," Trixi said. She hovered above Ellie's shoulder. "It just needed a bit of pixie magic to help it along," she added in a whisper.

Ellie giggled.

As the king led everyone farther into the courtyard, they passed a huge fountain surrounded by a cloud of sweet-smelling bubbles.

"Hang on a minute," said Jasmine. "That's not water, is it?"

Trixi smiled. "No. It's lemonade!"

"A lemonade fountain!" Ellie cried, running back and forth, trying to catch one of the fragrant bubbles on her tongue. Summer and Jasmine laughed as they watched their friend.

Behind them came the *clip-clop* of hooves, and they turned to see a beautiful blue pony led by an elf butler, which was pulling a wagon loaded with brightly wrapped packages.

"My birthday presents!" King Merry exclaimed excitedly.

But Summer wasn't interested in the gifts. She couldn't take her eyes off the pony and its aquamarine mane.

"He's gorgeous." She smiled.

"And he looks really friendly," Ellie added, staring into the pony's warm brown eyes.

Smiling, Trixi tapped her pixie ring and a rosy-red apple appeared in each girl's palm. But just as they started feeding them to the pony, Jasmine felt a chill suddenly crawl up her neck. A dark shadow fell over the courtyard.

"Oh no!" cried King Merry. He pointed to the sky.

Floating over the palace was an enormous thundercloud. On top of the ugly gray cloud the girls could see a tall, thin woman with a spiky silver crown and a mess of frizzy black hair.

"Oh no," Trixi whispered. "Queen Malice is here!"

Party Games

Jasmine, Ellie, and Summer stared up
at Queen Malice on her cloud, their
hearts beating fast. Lightning crackled
all around, giving the girls the shivers.
Thunder rumbled loudly as the cloud
stopped above King Merry's palace just
long enough for a burst of rain to pour
right onto his presents.

"Your birthday party is ruined, brother!" Queen Malice shouted at King Merry. "Just you wait and see!"

"What do you think she did?" Summer asked the others. But neither Ellie nor Jasmine could guess.

Queen Malice gave a cackle of mocking laughter, then the gray cloud sped off.

Suddenly the presents in the wagon began to shake and rustle. There was the sound of tearing as little legs pushed through the wrapping paper. Then the gifts leapt from the cart and ran away!

"My presents!" King Merry wailed.

Trixi tapped her ring. Although a stream of purple glitter flowed from it, nothing happened to the gifts. "My pixie magic isn't strong enough to undo Queen Malice's spells!" she cried.

Without thinking, Ellie dived forward and caught one of the escaping gifts. As soon as she did, the legs disappeared and the present sat innocently in her hands.

"Quick," Jasmine said. "We've got to catch the rest!"

Everyone leapt after the fleeing gifts. Jasmine and Summer managed to herd three into a corner and pick them up. One ran straight through the legs of a surprised-looking elf butler. Ellie, who was following it, couldn't stop in time and knocked him over! King Merry caught one by jumping on it, and then looked sadly at the present, which was now squashed flat.

"At least I can fix that," Trixi told him, tapping her ring and repairing it magically.

Eventually all the presents were caught and changed back to normal. The girls stacked them back on the wagon.

Trixi blew her hair out of her eyes. "I wish we could find a way to stop Queen Malice once and for all," she said fiercely.

"And her horrible helpers, the Storm Sprites. The queen has all kinds of mean tricks up her sleeve, and we never know where she'll turn up next."

"She is such a bully," said King Merry. "And she's determined to ruin my birthday. I just know that cursed thunderbolt of hers is hidden here somewhere, all ready to cause trouble." The king's eyes brimmed with tears. "This is going to be the worst party ever — my subjects are going to be miserable, and they won't have any fun."

"Yes, they will," Ellie said, her eyes flashing. "Because we're going to find the thunderbolt and stop it from doing any harm!"

"That's right," Summer and Jasmine chorused in loud, firm voices.

"And I'll help, too," Trixi said, floating up to the king's face and drying his tears away.

"Thank you, girls," said King Merry, but his voice was still shaky.

"Bobbins!" Trixi called to one of the elf butlers.

The elf rushed over and bowed deeply.

"King Merry needs a cup of hot cocoa with extra marshmallows," Trixi explained. "And then he needs to change into his party clothes. His guests will be arriving in two hours!"

Bobbins led the king away into the palace.

"Let's go and find that thunderbolt!" Trixi said as she dusted off her hands. "We should start in the palace gardens, since that's where the guests will gather later. Remember to keep an eye out for trouble!"

She stood up on her leaf and sped ahead, leading the girls out of the courtyard and into a maze with twisting and turning paths that seemed to change every time they blinked. Summer, Ellie, and Jasmine looked down every path and under all the hedges, but there was no sign of the thunderbolt anywhere.

Trixi led them out of the maze and past a beautiful pond that had a rainbow leading down into its depths. Trixi explained that the rainbow was a magical slide that could take you anywhere in the Secret Kingdom you wanted to go.

Finally, the girls walked into a garden filled with trees made of cotton candy.

Bunting hung from the trees, and a group of brownies were busy putting lots of cakes onto a long table.

"These ones look amazing," Ellie said, pointing to a cluster of pink-frosted cupcakes.

"They're cupcakes," Trixi explained.

"Oh, we have those at home," Jasmine said, sounding a bit disappointed.

"Really?" Trixi said. "The magical kind? If you eat one, you'll be able to fly for five minutes!"

"Wow!" Jasmine exclaimed. "We definitely don't have cupcakes like that! Can we try them?"

Trixi nodded. "Just one bite, though, we don't want the magic lasting too long. We've got a thunderbolt to find!"

Jasmine grinned excitedly and offered

the cupcakes to her friends, but Ellie shook her head. "Flying like a fairy? No thanks, I'm happy to have my feet on the ground!"

Jasmine took a small bite of her cupcake. After a moment's hesitation, Summer did the same. Instantly, a pair of glittering wings sprang out on each of their backs.

Jasmine flapped her wings carefully, and then shot upward. Summer was soon beside her and they zoomed through the air, going higher and higher. The wind whipped through their hair as they did loop-the-loops and whooped with excitement.

Trixi twirled in the air with them, and then came to land on Ellie's shoulder. "Don't go too high up," she called to Jasmine and Summer.

Just as Trixi spoke, Summer began to wobble. "Uh-oh, my wings are shrinking!" she cried out.

"Jasmine, look out!" Ellie shouted as her friend's wings disappeared.

"Don't worry, Ellie," Trixi said. She tapped her ring and Jasmine and Summer suddenly slowed and landed gently on the ground.

"Whew!" Jasmine said, then grinned. "That was so much fun!"

Trixi winked at the girls. "Flying with leaves is much safer." She giggled.

Summer chuckled, although her legs still felt wobbly. "I think you're right!"

At the other end of the table, Ellie
pointed to some heart-shaped treats.
"Hey, what are these called?"

"Endless cookies," a brownie piped up.
He only came up to Ellie's knee. He was
covered in soft brown hair and wore a
funny green cap. "You can eat as many as
you want and never get full. Would you
like one?"

"Yes, please!" Ellie took one and popped
it into her mouth. "Yum! It tastes like
strawberries and chocolate and ice cream
all rolled into one!"

Trixi and the girls continued to look
around the palace grounds, searching for
any sign of Queen Malice's thunderbolt
or the problems it might be causing, but
there was still no trace of it. Eventually

they reached an orchard where party games were being set up.

They could see a large barrel where seven dwarfs were practicing bobbing for golden apples. Nearby, two tiny pixie girls were busy wrapping one of their friends in glittery pink paper.

"What are they doing?" Summer asked.

"They're getting ready to play Pass the Pixie, of course!" Trixi said. "It's a great honor to be chosen as the pixie in the package."

Ellie grinned as she spotted a cheeky-
looking imp drawing a unicorn on a
wall. When the picture was complete, the
unicorn stamped its hooves and nodded
its regal head.

"Let me guess." She smiled. "Pin the Tail on the Unicorn?"

Trixi nodded. "We'll also have Musical Thrones and Blind Brownie's Bluff. Then, of course, there's Musical Statues, but I've made the gnomes promise to change the guests back to normal right after the game is finished this time." Trixi shook her head. "It's really no fun being a statue for too long — I hate staying still!"

Ellie and Jasmine laughed, but Summer's forehead creased with worry. "What are we going to do? The party starts soon, and we still haven't found the thunderbolt."

"We just have to keep looking," Trixi said. "We know it has to be somewhere around the palace. Malice's nasty magic will reveal itself soon enough."

Suddenly, a loud burst of laughter whipped through the air.

"What was that?" Ellie asked urgently. "Is it Queen Malice?"

Trixi crinkled her little brow. "No, it didn't sound like her."

The wild laugh sounded again.

"It's coming from over there," Summer said, pointing to an iron gate with ivy curling over the top.

"That's the Outdoor Theater, where the king's royal performers are putting on a show to begin the birthday celebrations," Trixi said, flying toward the arched entrance. "Come on, we need to find out what's happening!"

Ellie, Summer, and Jasmine raced toward the archway and then stopped in horror. There, sticking in the ground next to the entrance, was a jagged black thunderbolt!

Malice's Nasty Surprise

As Ellie, Summer, and Jasmine stared at Queen Malice's horrible thunderbolt, another loud laugh came from the theater.

"We have to find out what trouble the thunderbolt's caused," Ellie exclaimed.

"At least someone sounds happy. . . ." Summer said hopefully.

They stepped through the gates. Rows of marble seats led down to a wide stage. All around them, performers lay in heaps, tears streaming from their eyes.

"We've got the — hee-hee — the g-g-giggles," a leprechaun managed to squeak between screeches of laughter. "A-a-and we don't know why!" The little man held his aching sides. "The sh-show — hee-hee-hee — starts in half an hour, and all of our scenery has been covered with black paint."

Trixi looked angry. "Queen Malice," she hissed. "She's trying to ruin the show." She tapped her ring and chanted a spell:

"With this magic, hear my plea,
Stop laughing and act normally!"

A shower of purple glitter spread through the air and settled on the performers. But they still couldn't stop laughing.

"Malice's magic is much too powerful for me. We're going to have to cancel the performance." Trixi shook her head in despair. "It was supposed to be the grand opening to the party. King Merry's palace is usually full of laughter — and Queen Malice has turned that into a bad thing. King Merry will be heartbroken."

"Wait," Jasmine said. "We can't let Queen Malice win. Maybe magic isn't the only way to stop her."

"What do you mean, Jasmine?" Summer asked.

"The four of us can put on the show ourselves," Jasmine announced.

Ellie nodded, a smile stretching across her face. "If you can get me some paint and brushes," she said, "I can easily paint some new scenery."

"And I can write you a song to perform, Jasmine," Summer offered.

Jasmine glanced over at the giggling performers. "I think we'll need a dance as well. I can make something up."

Trixi's face bloomed with happiness. "And I'll help you all in any way I can! First, paint and brushes!" Trixi tapped her ring and instantly several brushes and pots of bright colors appeared.

Ellie knelt down and gathered them up. "Perfect!" She hurried over to the stage, stepping over a giggling elf. There were six backdrops at the rear of the stage. Ellie shook her head in disgust as she saw that they had all been covered with big splashes of black paint.

Ellie squeezed her eyes shut and tried to remember all the wonderful places she'd seen from the back of her swan. In no time at all she had painted a whole new scene showing the mermaids she had seen in the beautiful greenish-blue sea.

"One down, five to go," Ellie said to herself determinedly.

Meanwhile, Jasmine had started practicing some tricky dance moves. Her face was serious as she concentrated on making the steps as polished as possible.

Summer chewed on a pencil as she tried to think of lyrics for a new song. She looked up at the sky, hoping that the words might jump into her head. Her eyes widened. Even though it was daytime and the sun was shining, she could also see shooting stars and the moon glowing brightly in the sky. She blinked as she saw a face appear in the white surface of the moon and wink down at her. Summer smiled and eagerly scribbled something down. She knew exactly what the song's chorus would be!

Trixi whizzed between the girls, helping out where she could. Finally, the scenery, dance, and song were all finished.

"We've sorted out the show, but what about the poor performers?" kindhearted Summer asked. She nodded at the actors, stagehands, and musicians, who were still lying on the ground giggling.

"At least they're happy!" Trixi smiled as an elf gave a squeal of laughter. "But we need to get them backstage — and quickly! The king's guests will be here soon." She tapped her ring and conjured up some floating stretchers, which carried off the giggling performers. Trixi and the girls quickly followed them.

From the wings of the stage, they watched as the guests took their seats. The audience let out a huge cheer as King Merry arrived, wearing his ceremonial robes, which were so long they almost tripped him as he walked!

Trixi floated behind him, holding up the end of his robes like a wedding dress as he made his way to his seat, looking very excited.

Trixi tapped her ring and two spotlights burst to life. "It's showtime!" she said.

Jasmine took a deep breath and marched out onto the stage. She felt braver when she saw Ellie's beautiful backdrops, with their paintings of mermaids, glittering golden beaches, and snowcapped mountains.

From the wings, Summer and Ellie peered into the crowd. They had never seen an audience like it. To the right, there were two real-life unicorns. To the left, a group of fairies with bright shimmering wings whispered excitedly. In the front row were the youngest pixies, elves, dwarfs, and imps.

On the stage, Jasmine didn't have long to take it all in. She had to start the show.

"Thank you for coming here from all over the Secret Kingdom," Jasmine called out. "Welcome to the start of King Merry's birthday party!" She threw her arms wide, just as she'd seen performers do on TV. The audience cheered in approval. Whispers rippled through the crowd.

Trixi grinned at Summer and Ellie. "The crowd loves her! I don't think they've ever seen a human girl before."

"We have quite a show for you tonight,"
Jasmine continued. "But first I must tell
you about something that almost stopped
it from going ahead at all."

King Merry's face went pale, but
Jasmine caught his eye and winked
reassuringly. She swiftly explained how

Queen Malice's magic had given the royal performers a bad case of the giggles and damaged the scenery.

"My friends Summer, Ellie, Trixi, and I have put together a new show for you!" Jasmine said with a flourish. "We're not going to let Queen Malice ruin the king's birthday, are we?"

"NOOOOO!" the crowd roared.

"That's the spirit!" Jasmine said, beaming at the crowd. "We have a very special song for the king. But before I start, I think I need some backup singers. Summer and Ellie, will you come out and join me?"

Summer felt her cheeks go warm. She reached up quickly to twirl one of her braids. "I can't perform in front of all those people," she whispered.

"Yes, you can," Ellie urged. "Come on!" She dragged Summer onto the stage, and Trixi conjured up microphones for them both.

Jasmine grinned at her friends. "Trixi? Hit it!"

Trixi tapped her ring, and all at once the instruments floated up from the sides of the stage and began to play a cheerful melody. With one more burst of glitter from Trixi's ring, another sparkly microphone appeared in the air, and Jasmine caught it.

The three girls began to sing Summer's song. It was all about the Secret Kingdom and the places the king loved best. The audience thought it was wonderful and soon started singing along with the chorus:

"The Secret Kingdom
is a magical place,
Even the moon has a smiley face.
The king's birthday will
be a day of fun,
Malice's meanness will be undone."

While the instruments kept playing,
Jasmine handed her microphone to Ellie
and began her
dance routine.
Her dark
hair
whipped
all around
her as she
skipped
across the
stage.

The crowd clapped wildly in approval.

Ellie gave Summer a big grin. "We've done it. We've stopped Queen Malice from ruining the party and —"

SPLAT!

Ellie was interrupted by something hitting the scenery.

She and Summer looked up. Six strange-looking creatures with spiky hair, batlike wings, and ugly faces had swooped down into the open-air theater, riding on mini thunderclouds. Their eyes were shining with mischief and their mouths were twisted into angry scowls.

Jasmine hadn't noticed them yet because she was far too

busy dancing. But Summer could see that in their hands they held big fat raindrops, which they began hurling toward the stage!

"Trixi!" Summer hissed, beckoning to the pixie, who was hovering nearby. "Who are they?"

"Oh no!" Trixi's face fell. "Those are Storm Sprites, Queen Malice's servants." The pixie looked worried. "And if we get hit by one of their misery drops, we'll be made as sad and mean as she is."

"We've got to stop them!" Ellie cried.

Summer nodded and looked over at Jasmine. A misery drop was whizzing straight toward her!

Ducking and Diving

"Jasmine!" shouted Summer. "Duck!"

Jasmine heard the warning just in time and dove to the ground as the misery drop sailed over her head, missing her by inches. Immediately she jumped back to her feet and tap-danced on the spot, trying to keep the show going.

"Those are Queen Malice's Storm Sprites!" Ellie called to her, pointing up at the sky toward where the creatures were hovering.

Trixi flew over to Jasmine. "We have to get off the stage. Getting hit by one of those misery drops would be really bad news."

Jasmine kept on tap-dancing. "We can't stop," she said. "We can't let them ruin everything!"

From the stage, Ellie and Summer saw King Merry fall out of his chair as he dodged one of the Storm Sprites' misery drops.

Drops were now splashing into the audience, causing little rain clouds to spring up over everyone's heads. Soon unicorns, pixies, and elves were all looking miserable.

Up on the stage, Jasmine began to dance faster. "Hey, sprites!" she called. "Bet you can't get me!"

The six Storm Sprites narrowed their eyes and flew toward her.

"We're going to soak you!" one of the sprites said with a sneer. "Splish, splash, splosh!" He hurled a misery drop at Jasmine, but she jumped out of the way.

"Careful!" another sprite screeched. "You almost got me." The two sprites began to argue.

"That's it!" Jasmine said to herself. "If we can get the sprites to throw the drops at one another, we can turn their magic back on them!"

"Jasmine, come on!" Summer called as she and Ellie dodged and dived to avoid the misery drops splattered around them. "Duck!"

But Jasmine stood absolutely still.

"Jasmine, what are you doing?" Ellie called.

"Quick, get beside me and wait for my shout," Jasmine said. To her left she could see three Storm Sprites whizzing toward her on their rain clouds, misery drops raised. Another three were coming at her from the right. Ellie and Summer raced over to stand next to her.

"They're going to splash us!" Ellie cried.

"One . . . two . . . three . . . DUCK!" Jasmine shouted.

All three girls dropped to the ground
just as all the sprites released their misery
drops. There was a great *SPLAT*, and then
a series of loud wails. All six sprites had
been hit, and each one was soaking wet!
Little storm clouds broke out over each
sprite's head.

"Ugh!" one sprite whined. "I'm all cold and wet! I've got water up my nose. Look, I can blow bubbles."

"Me too," said the sprite next to him, letting all his drops fall to the ground and sitting on his cloud gloomily.

Jasmine rushed forward, scooped up his misery drops, and passed some to Summer and Ellie.

"Take that!" she yelled as they pelted the Storm Sprites with misery drops.

"Argh!" yelled a sprite. "This is horrible. Let's get out of here!"

The sprites' rain clouds rose into the air and zoomed quickly out of sight.

"Yes!" Jasmine cheered. "We did it!"

Ellie jumped up and down in delight.

But Summer was staring at the misery drop in her hands with a twinkle in her eye. "I have an idea," she whispered. "Maybe the misery drops can cure the performers' giggles."

"Let's ask Trixi," Jasmine suggested, waving her over.

The little pixie was helping King Merry, who had been hit with a misery drop and was sitting unhappily in a puddle with a cloud raining down on his head.

"He's so sad!" Trixi sighed as she flew over to the girls.

Summer quickly explained her plan and Trixi's eyes shone brightly. "Good idea, Summer!"

Summer held out the shining droplet,

and Trixi pointed at it. Her pixie ring
gleamed as she chanted:

"Go to the performers, misery drop,
And make their silly laughing stop!"

The drop vanished, and there was a loud
cracking sound from outside the theater.

"What was that noise?" Summer asked,
pulling her two friends to their feet.

"I think I know," said Trixi. She darted
to the theater gates, and reappeared with
a mass of ugly black splinters floating
behind her in a cloud of dust. "They're
from Queen Malice's thunderbolt," she
explained.

"Yuck!" Summer said, peering at the
splinters. "Even now, it still looks nasty.
But what happened to it?"

"When you girls helped the performers and stopped Queen Malice from ruining the show, it broke her spell," explained Trixi. "And the thunderbolt must have shattered."

Trixi tapped her ring and the splinters disappeared in a puff of smoke.

An angry shriek sounded, and suddenly a storm cloud appeared overhead with a familiar figure on top. It was Queen Malice, shaking her bony fist. "You human girls may have broken my first thunderbolt," she screeched, "but next time you won't be so lucky. My next one is hidden so well that you'll never find it!" She threw her head back and laughed as she zoomed away on her cloud.

Trixi shuddered.

"Don't worry, Trixi," Jasmine said fiercely. "We won't let her ruin the Secret Kingdom."

The others nodded.

"Oh, look." Summer smiled. "The performers — they've all stopped laughing."

Everyone turned to watch the royal performers walking out onto the stage. They were all shaking their heads as if waking up from a bad dream.

In the audience, the rain clouds had disappeared from above King Merry and the rest of the audience, and they all looked happy once again.

"Now that the thunderbolt is broken, all of Queen Malice's mean magic is undone!" Trixi said happily.

"Great," Jasmine said with a grin. "Now that everyone's back to normal, we can do a grand finale to the show!" She turned to the audience. "Sorry about the interruption, everybody. I think we should all sing along for this one. Are you ready?"

The crowd cheered. Jasmine whispered something to Trixi, and the little pixie tapped her ring. The instruments immediately struck up a familiar tune, and the whole audience sang "Happy Birthday" to King Merry. His face broke into a smile and tears of joy rolled down his plump cheeks.

After the show had finished, King Merry

came backstage to congratulate Summer, Jasmine, and Ellie.

"If it weren't for them, Sire, we would never have destroyed Queen Malice's thunderbolt," Trixi said.

The King smiled. "The Magic Box was very wise indeed when it took us to the girls. Summer, Jasmine, and Ellie, will you continue to be friends to the Secret Kingdom, and help stop my sister from causing more trouble?"

"Definitely," said Jasmine.

"I can't wait to come back!" Ellie grinned.

"We'll be here anytime you need us," added Summer.

The king nodded. "But you must promise to keep the Secret Kingdom a secret."

"We promise," Jasmine vowed. King Merry nodded at Trixi, and she grinned and tapped her pixie ring.

Suddenly, out of nowhere, three beautiful tiaras appeared in the air above the girls! Each one was surrounded by a sparkling glow. Summer's was a delicate rosy-gold color, with beautiful pink, heart-shaped jewels. Ellie's had fancy swirls and a green, diamond-shaped jewel in the center. Jasmine's was a shimmering gold with intricate loops and pretty opals that seemed to sparkle with all the colors of the rainbow.

The girls gasped as the tiaras settled carefully on top of their heads. They fitted perfectly!

King Merry smiled. "These tiaras will appear whenever you are here, and they will show everyone that you are VIFs of the Secret Kingdom, on important royal business."

"VIFs?" Jasmine wondered out loud.

"Very Important Friends," Trixi whispered.

"Wow!" said Ellie, taking her tiara off to look at it. "This is the most beautiful thing I've ever seen!"

Jasmine and Summer smiled broadly as they looked at each other's tiaras. "Thank you so much, King Merry!"

Trixi smiled at the girls and did a little somersault of delight. "I'm so pleased that you will visit us again," she said. "I'll be here to guide you every step of the way. And this will help as well."

Trixi pointed her ring toward the beautiful pictures of the Secret Kingdom that Ellie had painted as backdrops for the show. As the girls watched, the pictures flew up into the air in a burst of twinkles. And as they floated down, the pictures joined together and grew smaller and smaller, then landed in Summer's hands.

"It's a map of the Secret Kingdom!" Summer exclaimed.

But as the girls looked at the map closely, they realized that it wasn't an ordinary map — it was moving! The sea around the island had blue waves that lapped against the shore. The trees of the forests swayed in a breeze, and the meadows of sunflowers gleamed.

"There are five more of Queen Malice's nasty thunderbolts somewhere in the kingdom, just waiting to cause trouble," Trixi continued. "The Magic Box will tell you when it has located one, and the map will help you find out where it is."

The girls nodded. "We'll be back whenever we're needed," Summer promised.

"Good-bye, girls," Trixi said, flying up to kiss each of them on the tip of her nose. "See you very soon!"

With a tap of her ring, Trixi conjured up a whirlwind that scooped the girls up into the air, higher and higher. Then, with a bright flash of light, they found themselves landing gently back in Summer's bedroom.

Jasmine stared down at the Magic Box, which was still sitting on the fluffy white rug, exactly where they had left it.

"Did all that just happen, or was I having a strange dream?" she said. She put her hand up to feel for her tiara, but it was gone.

"It really happened," Summer breathed. "Look!" She held up the map of the kingdom.

"Where should we keep it?" Ellie asked. "It'll have to be somewhere secret. You heard what King Merry said — nobody can know about the Secret Kingdom except us."

As she spoke, the mirror on the Magic Box glowed. Then, to the girls' amazement, the box slowly opened, revealing six little wooden compartments,

all of different sizes! A shower of light
sparkled from the center of the box.

"It's the perfect place to store our gift!"
Summer exclaimed.

Ellie gently placed the folded map into
one of the spaces. It fitted perfectly! As
soon as the map was in place, the lid on
the box closed again.

"I wonder when the Magic Box will tell

us that it's time for our next adventure," said Jasmine.

"I hope it's soon," Summer said, crossing her fingers.

Ellie looked at the mirrored lid of the Magic Box and for a moment thought she saw King Merry's kind face beaming out at her.

"The Secret Kingdom needs us," she said softly. "I have a feeling we'll be back there very soon."

Character Profile:
Ellie
Macdonald

Family:

Ellie lives with her parents and little sister, Molly.

Favorite Colors:

Green and purple

Loves:

Painting and drawing

Favorite Place in the Secret Kingdom:

Mermaid Reef

Personality:

Quirky and creative. When everyone else is baffled by a problem, Ellie is often the one to find a brilliant solution.

Character Quiz

Jasmine, Ellie, and Summer are all heroes! But which one are you most like? Take our quiz to find out.

A baby bird has fallen out of its nest! Do you . . . ?

A — Take it home and look after it. You can't bear to see an animal in pain.

B — Climb back up the tree and put it in its nest.

C — Run for help — you really want to get the bird back to its nest, but you're not going up there!

Everyone's performing in a talent show! What would your talent be?

A — You couldn't possibly perform in front of people — you'll help backstage.

B — Singing and dancing — you want to be the star of the show!

C — Painting.

What's your favorite color?

A — Sunshine yellow.

B — Hot pink.

C — Purple and green.

What's your favorite hobby?

A — Visiting the pet store to see all the cuddly animals.

B — Going to dance class.

C — Designing your own clothes.

Which personality traits best describe you?

A — Shy and quiet.

B — Outgoing and energetic.

C — Funny and clever.

Mostly As

You are Summer!
You are kind and thoughtful,
and you love animals!
You're sometimes a little
bit quieter than your friends,
but you still love hanging
out with them and
having fun in the
Secret Kingdom.

Mostly Bs

You are Jasmine! You are
brave and energetic. You
love being the center of
attention, especially when it
comes to singing
and dancing.

Mostly Cs

You are Ellie! You are funny
and clever, and you're
artistic, too! Even though
you're scared of heights,
you're brave enough to do
things that scare you.

The Rescue Princesses

These are no ordinary princesses—
they're Rescue Princesses!

RAINBOW magic

These activities are magical!
Play dress-up, send friendship notes, and much more!

SCHOLASTIC
www.scholastic.com
www.rainbowmagiconline.com

HiT entertainment

RMACTIV3

RAINBOW magic™

SPECIAL EDITION

Which Magical Fairies Have You Met?

3 stories in each one!

- ☐ Joy the Summer Vacation Fairy
- ☐ Holly the Christmas Fairy
- ☐ Kylie the Carnival Fairy
- ☐ Stella the Star Fairy
- ☐ Shannon the Ocean Fairy
- ☐ Trixie the Halloween Fairy
- ☐ Gabriella the Snow Kingdom Fairy
- ☐ Juliet the Valentine Fairy
- ☐ Mia the Bridesmaid Fairy
- ☐ Flora the Dress-Up Fairy
- ☐ Paige the Christmas Play Fairy
- ☐ Emma the Easter Fairy
- ☐ Cara the Camp Fairy
- ☐ Destiny the Rock Star Fairy
- ☐ Belle the Birthday Fairy
- ☐ Olympia the Games Fairy
- ☐ Selena the Sleepover Fairy
- ☐ Cheryl the Christmas Tree Fairy
- ☐ Florence the Friendship Fairy
- ☐ Lindsay the Luck Fairy
- ☐ Brianna the Tooth Fairy
- ☐ Autumn the Falling Leaves Fairy
- ☐ Keira the Movie Star Fairy
- ☐ Addison the April Fool's Day Fairy

■ SCHOLASTIC

Find all of your favorite fairy friends at
scholastic.com/rainbowmagic

HiT entertainment

RMSPECIAL12

RAINBOW magic™

Which Magical Fairies Have You Met?

- ☐ The Rainbow Fairies
- ☐ The Weather Fairies
- ☐ The Jewel Fairies
- ☒ The Pet Fairies
- ☒ The Dance Fairies
- ☒ The Music Fairies
- ☐ The Sports Fairies
- ☒ The Party Fairies
- ☐ The Ocean Fairies
- ☐ The Night Fairies
- ☒ The Magical Animal Fairies
- ☐ The Princess Fairies
- ☐ The Superstar Fairies
- ☐ The Fashion Fairies
- ☒ The Sugar & Spice Fairies

■ SCHOLASTIC

Find all of your favorite fairy friends at
scholastic.com/rainbowmagic

RMFAIRY9

Caterpillar Maze

Jasmine, Ellie, and Summer need to get the slime
caterpillars to the racetrack. Can you help
them find their way through the maze?
Watch out for Storm Sprites!

Personality:

Quiet, thoughtful, and caring. If someone's upset, Summer will be the one to notice and help them.

Favorite Color:

Yellow.

Loves:

Animals and reading.

Favorite Place in the Secret Kingdom:

Unicorn Valley. The baby unicorns are so cute!

Family:

Summer has one older brother, Phoenix, and two younger brothers, Finn and Connor. They all live with their mother and stepfather.

Character Profile:
Summer Hammond

Unicorn Valley

ISBN 978-0545-66769-2

All rights reserved. Published by Scholastic Inc., 557 Broadway, New York, NY 10012 by arrangement with Orchard Books. SCHOLASTIC and associated logos are trademarks and/or registered trademarks of Scholastic Inc.

12 11 10 9 8 7 6 5 4 3 2 1   14 15 16 17 18 19/0

Printed in the U.S.A.   40
This edition first printing, January 2014

Secret Kingdom

Unicorn Valley

ROSIE BANKS

Scholastic Inc.

Contents

A New Adventure

"There!" said Ellie Macdonald, standing back to admire the pretty shapes laid out on the baking tray.

It was a rainy Sunday afternoon and her best friends, Summer Hammond and Jasmine Smith, had come over to bake cookies. Summer had designed hers in the shape of hearts, while Jasmine had made crowns. Artistic Ellie had created cookie fairies.

"How long do we bake them for?" asked Summer, twirling one of her blond braids thoughtfully. "I don't want them to burn!"

"Fifteen minutes," said Ellie, consulting the cookbook.

"Fifteen minutes!" wailed Jasmine dramatically, slumping down in her chair so that her glossy black hair flew around her face. "But I'm starving!"

"It'll go by in a flash." Ellie giggled. "I'll get the timer."

She jumped up from the table where they had been working, then stumbled as she caught her foot on the leg of her chair.

"Oops," she said as it clattered to the floor.

Mrs. Macdonald came in to see what

the noise was. "Don't you worry, girls,"
she said, admiring the cookies. "I'll put
these in to bake, and call you when
they're done. I'm sure they'll be delicious.
And you've made such lovely shapes!
Crowns and hearts and even fairies. What
imaginations you all have."

While Mrs. Macdonald was
putting the cookies into the
oven, the three friends
exchanged a grin. Of
course Ellie's mom
thought they had
good imaginations —
she hadn't been to
the Secret Kingdom, the
magical land where only
a few days ago the girls had
actually met a real king wearing a real

crown, seen fairies, and eaten magical heart-shaped endless cookies at King Merry's birthday party!

"Let's go upstairs while the cookies are baking," suggested Jasmine loudly. "And check on the Magic Box," she added quietly as the girls headed up to Ellie's room. "Just in case! You did bring it, didn't you, Summer?"

"Of course," Summer said with a smile.

Ellie's bedroom was long and light, with her art books and tools scattered across a big desk and the colorful pictures she'd painted pinned all over the lilac walls.

The girls settled down on the big window seat where Ellie did her painting. Summer carefully pulled the Magic Box out of her bag and passed it to Jasmine, who stared eagerly at its mirrored lid.

The box was just as beautiful as when they had first found it. Its wooden sides were delicately carved with images of magical creatures, and its curved lid had a mirror surrounded by six glittering green stones.

"It was so lucky we found this at the school rummage sale." Summer smiled.

"We didn't find it — it found us!" Jasmine reminded her. "The Magic Box knew we were the only ones who could help the Secret Kingdom."

The Secret Kingdom was an amazing place where lots of magical creatures lived — but it had a big problem. Ever since its subjects had chosen King Merry to rule instead of his nasty sister, Queen Malice, Malice had been determined to make everyone in the kingdom as miserable as she was. She'd scattered six horrible thunderbolts around the land, and each of them contained a spell to cause lots of trouble.

"The kingdom still needs our help, though," said Ellie. "We stopped Queen Malice's first thunderbolt from wrecking King Merry's birthday party, but we've only found one of the thunderbolts she hid. Trixibelle said there were six."

"I hope we see Trixi again soon," said

Summer. "It was so wonderful meeting a real pixie."

"Well, it doesn't look like we'll be seeing her today," said Jasmine sadly, putting the Magic Box down and flopping onto Ellie's homemade rag rug. "The mirror's blank."

"No, it isn't!" exclaimed Ellie, grabbing the box and leaning over it. "Look!"

The mirror was starting to glimmer and shine. Words began to float up from its shimmering depths.

"It's a riddle!" said Ellie. She read the words in the mirror out loud:

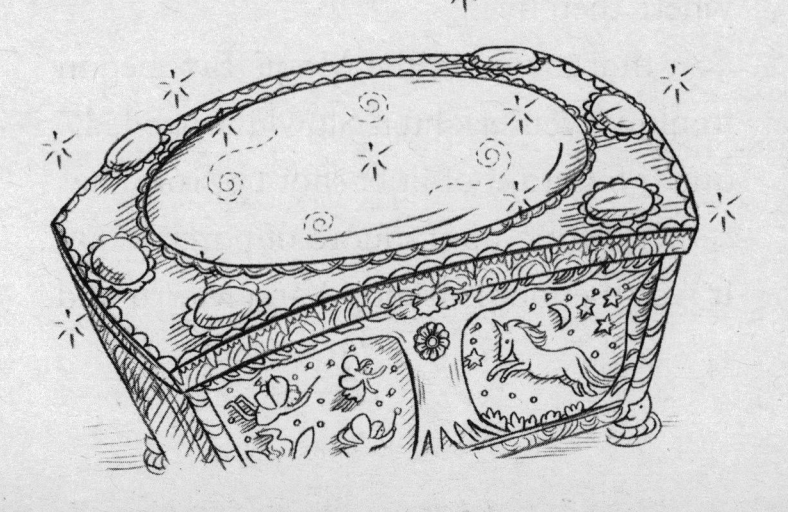

"The second thunderbolt is found
Where one-horned creatures
Walk the ground.
Its wicked magic must be foiled
Before a special game is spoiled!"

Ellie crinkled her forehead thoughtfully. "Creatures with one horn," she said. "I don't know about you, but that makes me think of . . ."

"Unicorns!" broke in Summer, her eyes shining. "There were unicorns at King Merry's birthday party! But I don't know where they live."

At that moment, the Magic Box began to glow even brighter. Slowly it opened, and a fountain of light shot up from the center, lifting up a square of parchment. It was the magical map King Merry had

given them after their last adventure!
Jasmine unfolded it carefully. It showed
the crescent moon–shaped island of the
Secret Kingdom. All three girls crowded
around the map.

"There's King Merry's palace," Jasmine said, pointing to the pink building with its four golden turrets. The flags at the top of the turrets waved slightly, as if in a breeze.

Summer was looking around the rest of the map. "Flower Forest," she read out. "Dolphin Bay."

"What's that?" asked Jasmine, pointing to a wooded area surrounded by steep hills.

Ellie looked closer. "Unicorn Valley!" she exclaimed. "That must be where the next thunderbolt is!"

They all looked at the Magic Box, but nothing happened.

"What did we do before?" Summer wondered aloud.

"We put our hands on the jewels, then Trixi and King Merry appeared!" Jasmine

remembered. The Magic Box started to glow again, and the friends rushed to press their palms onto the brilliant jewels.

"The answer to the riddle is Unicorn Valley!" Ellie whispered.

For a moment the light coming from the box flashed so brightly they had to shut their eyes. Then it died away, and everything was still.

The girls looked around cautiously.

"Do you think it worked?" asked Jasmine. "King Merry and Trixi appeared in Summer's wardrobe last time."

All three of them looked toward Ellie's wardrobe. Then, behind them, the lid of Ellie's toy chest started to rattle. . . .

Ellie saw it out of the corner of her eye and turned around so fast she almost fell

over. "They're stuck in the toy chest!" she cried.

"Don't worry," came a tinkly little voice from among the toys. "I'll be with you in a moment."

"Trixi!" the girls cried happily, recognizing the voice of King Merry's royal pixie, who had guided them around the Secret Kingdom during their last visit.

As they watched, pink petals began to creep around the edge of the lid of the chest. The flowers were growing magically fast, forcing it apart. The lid

burst open with a shower of petals and Trixi shot out, riding on a leaf. The tiny pixie waved at the girls excitedly, then tapped the magical ring she always wore. It sparkled and the magic flowers dissolved into glittery dust that settled on Ellie's floor before gradually fading away.

Then Trixi floated over to where the girls were standing. "It's lovely to see you again." She smiled, flying her leaf over to each of them in turn and kissing them on the nose.

"You, too," said Summer happily. After their last adventure it had hardly seemed real that they had made friends with a pixie, but here she was, looking just the same — her clothes made out of leaves, her messy blond hair peeking out from under her flower hat.

Trixi's blue eyes twinkled as she smiled at them all.

"But where's King Merry?" Jasmine asked.

"He's busy writing a speech," Trixi told her. "Every year the unicorns hold an event called the Golden Games and King Merry gives a welcome speech to everyone there. Except last time he got

confused and arrived at the end of the games, so I had to turn it into a good-bye speech instead!"

The girls all giggled. It was so nice to hear about the Secret Kingdom. But it was even better to go there and have adventures themselves!

"Poor King Merry." Jasmine laughed.

"Well, he might be in trouble again this year," said Ellie seriously. "The riddle says that Queen Malice's second thunderbolt is hidden in Unicorn Valley."

"Oh no!" exclaimed Trixi. "Let's see if we can spot it." She flew over the map and hovered over Unicorn Valley.

They looked down into an orchard full
of fruit trees, neat gardens, a steep hill
surrounded by multicolored grass, and
beautiful emerald-green fields.

"Unicorn Valley is one of the loveliest
spots in the kingdom," said Trixi. "Just
the sort of place Queen Malice would try
to wreck!"

"Well, we won't let her," said Ellie firmly.

"Let's go!" said Jasmine.

Trixi gave the Magic Box a tap with
her ring. Then she chanted:

*"The evil queen has trouble planned.
Brave helpers fly to save our land!"*

Trixi's words appeared on the mirrored
lid before streaming up to the ceiling.
They swirled around in a dancing cloud

and then surrounded the girls' heads in a glittering, flashing whirlwind.

"We're off to the Secret Kingdom!" cried Jasmine above the sound of rushing air.

The girls grabbed one another's hands as Ellie's bedroom seemed to drop away beneath them. There was a flash of blinding colors . . . and there, spread out below them just as they had been on the map, but much more beautiful, were the rolling green fields of Unicorn Valley.

Fields that were getting closer and closer very quickly!

"Aaarrgh!" shrieked Ellie, screwing her eyes shut. "We're falling!"

Into the Valley

"We're not falling, we're hang gliding!" called Jasmine from nearby.

Ellie realized that something was wrapped around her body, keeping her safe. She looked up and saw a huge red leaf, fluttering delicately above her head in the wind. Vines descended from it, looping safely around her waist.

"I think I can see all of Unicorn Valley," called Summer, who was drifting toward Ellie underneath a huge yellow leaf. In the center of the valley was an enormous tree that towered over all the others.

"That's the Great Apple Tree," said Trixi, who was flying along beside them on her own magical leaf. "It was the first tree that ever grew in Unicorn Valley."

"Um, it's lovely," said Ellie, a bit nervously. "But how do we land?"

"There's a patch of moss just down there," said Trixi. She pointed to a corner of a field filled with flowers. "That will work as a nice soft landing pad. Careful now!"

Flapping their arms and giggling, the girls steered their leaves down to land on the bouncy blue moss. Their leaves settled on top of them with a soft *flump* sound.

"Whew!" said Ellie from under her leaf, which had covered her like a collapsed tent. She pulled it off, but it caught something on her head. Ellie put up her hand to free it and realized she was wearing the beautiful tiara King Merry had given her at the end of their last adventure! She grinned and scrambled about, calling, "Trixi! Are you there?"

"I certainly am," said the little pixie.

Ellie climbed out from under her leaf, and nearly fell over in shock at what she saw. Two white unicorns were galloping gracefully toward them.

Their manes flowed in the wind and their horns sparkled in the sunshine — one silver and one gold. Ellie turned to look in wonder at Summer and Jasmine. Their tiaras had appeared magically on their heads, too, and they were both staring openmouthed at the beautiful creatures.

The bigger unicorn had a lovely wreath of braided leaves and berries resting on her mane. When she reached the girls, she stopped and gently touched the tip of her horn to each of their heads.

"That's a special sign of greeting," Trixi whispered to them. "You should curtsy."

Hastily, Summer and Ellie picked up the edges of their skirts and curtsied clumsily. Jasmine, who was wearing jeans, had to hold out the edges of her top.

"Welcome to Unicorn Valley," said the

unicorn in a regal voice. "I am Silvertail, leader of the unicorns, and this is my daughter, Littlehorn. You are the first humans I have seen in a long time."

The smaller unicorn whinnied. "I've *never* seen a human before," she said. She trotted around the girls, looking at them closely. "You haven't even got tails!" she said in disbelief.

Ellie and Jasmine giggled, but Summer was too awestruck. "I can't believe we're talking to real, live unicorns!" she whispered to Ellie.

Trixi flew her leaf around to hover in front of the girls, and cleared her throat. "Jasmine, Ellie, and Summer are honored guests of King Merry," she explained.

"We know," said Silvertail with a smile. She turned to face the girls. "We can tell from your tiaras that you are Very Important Friends of his. Everyone in the kingdom is talking about how you saved King Merry's birthday party from Queen Malice's nasty thunderbolt!" She shook her mane and harrumphed at the thought of the wicked queen.

"We think that another thunderbolt might have landed here in Unicorn

Valley," Ellie told her. "We have to find it before it causes any damage."

Silvertail whinnied anxiously. "My orchard keepers did say that there was something strange near the Great Apple Tree. I was on my way there when you arrived. Perhaps you should come with me?"

"Of course we will," Jasmine agreed.

"It'll be faster if you ride," Silvertail said, looking sideways at the girls' legs. "I will summon my strongest unicorns to carry you."

The three girls exchanged excited glances.

"We're going to ride on unicorns?" cried Jasmine.

Silvertail turned toward the fields and tossed her head. At once, three sturdy unicorns came galloping up. One was a

minty green, one was a deep midnight blue, and the last was a charcoal gray. All of them had long, dark manes and tails, and swirly, golden horns. Silvertail introduced them as Fleetfoot, Sleekmane, and Graycoat.

"We'll have a wonderful view from up here," said Jasmine, climbing onto Fleetfoot's mint-green back.

"But we're not too high!" said Ellie, settling onto Graycoat. "Just how I like it!"

"Thank you for carrying us," said Summer to Sleekmane. "This is the first time I've been on a unicorn."

"Hold on tight!" replied Sleekmane with a friendly whinny.

With Trixi hovering beside them, the friends followed Silvertail across Unicorn Valley.

"Have the unicorns always lived here?" asked Ellie.

"No," Silvertail explained. "Unicorn Valley was founded by a unicorn called Snowmane thousands of years ago. Back then, this whole area was covered with poisonous prickles and carnivorous plants. It was the wildest place in the whole kingdom. But then Snowmane touched a thornbush with her horn and turned it into a lovely magic apple tree. The tree spread its beauty out across the land, and all the awful plants disappeared."

Littlehorn swished her tail, cantering between her mother and the unicorns who carried the girls. "We look after the orchards and keep Unicorn Valley a magical place," she neighed happily.

"Those are the stables, where we sleep," said Silvertail, nodding toward a golden building that was set back from the road in a meadow full of flowers. "And up ahead you can see Happyhooves Academy, our school."

"Oh, the baby unicorns are *so* cute!" exclaimed Summer.

The group slowed down to admire the unicorn school, which was a big field divided into lots of open-air classrooms. Riding on their strong unicorn friends, Ellie, Jasmine, and Summer were soon close enough to see a teacher showing some very young unicorns how to write their names. Concentrating hard, they moved their horns through the air and glittery, floating letters appeared in front of them.

"Those little unicorns have silver horns, like you," said Summer to Littlehorn. "But all the big unicorns have gold horns."

"Our horns stay silver until we're grown up," explained Littlehorn. "Then we take part in the Golden Games and the elders turn our horns golden. You're here just at the right time — the games are this

afternoon! I'm competing in the Great
Race. The winner gets to be one of the
king's royal messengers and carry urgent
letters around the kingdom. It's a huge
honor!"

"I'm sure that's why the Magic Box
has called us now," Jasmine whispered in
Ellie's ear. "Queen Malice's thunderbolt is
going to wreck the Golden Games!"

"Not if we can help it!" Ellie replied
with a grin.

After a short trip, the girls trotted into
the orchards, where hundreds of neat trees
were being tended by older unicorns.

"This is the Royal Apple Orchard,"
Silvertail explained, "where all the apples
in the Secret Kingdom grow."

"Oh, I wish I had my art supplies so I
could draw it!" cried Ellie. "The orchard is

so lovely. . . . Or I could draw the stable. . . .
No, the baby unicorns!"

Silvertail smiled. "Come with me just
a little farther," she said, "and I will
show you the prettiest sight in the whole
valley."

Fleetfoot, Sleekmane, and Graycoat
cantered between two rows of neat trees
and came out in a clearing.

Right in the center was the enormous
tree the girls had seen as they glided into
the kingdom. It was even bigger close-up.

"Its trunk is as big as my house!" gasped
Jasmine.

The unicorns knelt so that Ellie,
Summer, and Jasmine could jump down
and walk over to the tree. Its ancient
branches stretched out above them, heavy
with gleaming apples.

"This is the Great Apple Tree that Snowmane created," said Silvertail. "Without it, Unicorn Valley would turn back into a wild and dark place."

"It's amazing!" breathed Ellie.

"This is where the orchard keepers said they saw something strange," said Silvertail. "Maybe the thunderbolt is hidden nearby."

The girls started looking all over the trunk of the tree. Trixi flew her leaf high up into the branches. But they couldn't see any sign of Queen Malice's thunderbolt.

Suddenly there was a whinny of alarm from the other side of the tree. Trixi gave the girls a worried glance, and they all ran around to see what was the matter.

Silvertail was there, staring at something stuck deep in the earth between the roots of the Great Apple Tree. It was a hard black shard that glistened horribly — the tip of Queen Malice's thunderbolt!

"Oh no!" Silvertail neighed urgently.

"Queen Malice's nasty thunderbolt is stuck in the roots of the Great Apple Tree! If the tree is hurt, its magic will disappear, and the whole valley will go back to being a wasteland!"

Slimy Caterpillars and Twisty Vines

The girls started inspecting the tree's lower branches to check for damage.

"I'll check the fruit," Littlehorn said. She concentrated hard, and with a wave of her horn an apple floated down from the top of the tree. It landed on the ground in front of her. Littlehorn nudged it with her horn and then froze.

"What's wrong?" Summer asked. As she watched, a lump rose on the apple's rosy skin. Then it burst — and out came the head of a big, purple, black-spotted caterpillar.

"That's a slime caterpillar!" Trixi cried. "They usually live on the other side of the kingdom, in the grounds of Queen

Malice's horrible Thunder Castle. The
more they eat, the bigger they get!"

The funny-looking
creature nosed around
in the warm air and
stuck its tongue
out at the girls
before burrowing
back out of sight.

"Yuck!" gasped
Ellie, stepping backward
into Littlehorn, who stumbled and
knocked over a basketful of apples.

The fruit spilled out onto the ground,
and more caterpillars fell out with it.

"Ugh, they're horrible!" said Jasmine,
looking at one of the slimy creatures,
which was chomping on an apple
enthusiastically.

Summer watched a caterpillar as it swallowed a big chunk of apple and then burped loudly. "They're just hungry," she said kindly.

"Summer, you'd love any animal — no matter how disgusting it is!" Ellie teased her friend.

"Let's see if I can get rid of them," said Trixi, guiding her leaf down next to the nearest caterpillar and tapping it with her ring. She chanted:

"You greedy things aren't wanted here.
This spell will make you disappear!"

Nothing happened.

"Queen Malice's magic is too strong for me." Trixi sighed.

The girls exchanged dismayed looks.

"We'll have to destroy the thunderbolt," Silvertail said. "I'll get my strongest unicorns and we'll pull it right out of the ground."

"It's no use," Trixi told her. "In order to get rid of the thunderbolt we'll have to break Queen Malice's spell."

"What will we do if the caterpillars hurt the tree?" Littlehorn asked. She was standing beneath the Great Apple Tree, gazing unhappily at the caterpillars, who were wriggling about among the spilled apples and chomping happily. A big, sparkling teardrop

rolled from one of her eyes. Where it splashed onto the grass, a tiny flower started to grow. "If the valley turns back the way it was, we'll have nowhere to go."

Silvertail looked at her daughter. "Why don't you go and practice for the race, Littlehorn?" she said kindly. "It'll take your mind off things. And you girls could all go and watch," she suggested, turning to Ellie, Summer, and Jasmine. "Maybe you'll be able to find more clues about what Queen Malice is up to, and how to stop her. My orchard keepers are the best gardeners in the Secret Kingdom. I'm sure they can take care of the caterpillars until we find out how to break Malice's spell. I'll stay here to help them."

"And I'll put a holding spell around the tree so that the caterpillars can't

spread to the rest of the orchard," Trixi told them.

"Yes, let's go to the practice area," Summer said to Littlehorn comfortingly, stroking her hand along the unicorn's coat. "We'll probably come up with an idea there."

The little unicorn nodded bravely and led the way out of the apple orchards, toward the racetrack. As they walked into the gardens, the girls looked around them anxiously, trying to spot any other signs of Queen Malice's mischief.

Summer noticed that Littlehorn was looking down at her hooves as she walked, with a worried expression on her face.

"Why don't you tell us about the Golden Games?" Summer asked to distract her.

The little unicorn looked happier at the thought of the afternoon's fun.

"Well, there's the Great Race, of course," she said. "And there are lots of other games and sports, and feats of unicorn magic, too."

"That sounds wonderful." Summer smiled as the girls reached the racetrack. It circled a playing field and a small hill, which was already crowded with unicorns watching the others practice. The track was covered with grass that grew in colored lines to show the runners where to go.

"What game are they playing?" asked Summer, pointing to some unicorns on the big field inside the track, who were leaping up at shining golden hoops that floated magically in the air and catching them on their horns.

"That's Unicorn-Horn Hoopla," said Littlehorn proudly. "And over there, they're playing a game of Runaway Rounders."

The girls watched a team of unicorns who were using their horns to hit a bright red ball. Every time the ball hit the ground it sprouted little legs and tried to run away from the fielders.

"Look, there's King Merry!" said Ellie, pointing excitedly. The little king looked very sharp in his royal robes, except that he had bits of paper sticking out of all his pockets, and ink stains on his cloak.

He was pacing up and down beside the track, scratching his head so hard that his half-moon spectacles were knocked almost off his nose.

"He looks worried," said Trixi. "I'd better see if he's okay."

Summer, Ellie, and Jasmine hurried over to the king, who was muttering to himself absentmindedly.

"Now, let me see," he said. "It is your honor to address me today. . . . Dearie me, no, that's not right. I mean, it is my honor to address you tomorrow. . . . Oh my goodness, no, that won't do either."

"Is he practicing his welcome speech?" Summer whispered to Trixi.

"I think he must be," replied the pixie. "He's not very good at remembering his lines!"

The king stopped pacing and patted his pockets as if he was looking for something. Trixi flew forward and conjured up a large spotted hanky, magicking his robes clean and tidy at the same time.

"Hello!" King Merry said cheerfully. "Girls, how nice to see you again. Are you here for the games?"

"Not quite," Ellie explained. "The Magic Box has brought us here. There's a thunderbolt in the roots of the Great Apple Tree."

"And it's already causing trouble," said Jasmine. "There are horrible slime caterpillars attacking the tree."

"How terrible!" said the king. "Do you have a plan to get rid of the thunderbolt?" He looked at the girls hopefully.

"Not yet," Ellie admitted. "But we're working on it."

"Wow, look at her go!" Summer said, pointing at Littlehorn, who was now racing around the colored track with five other young unicorns. "She's so fast!"

In spite of her worries, Summer couldn't help smiling as the beautiful creatures galloped along, urging one another on. "We won't let the unicorns down," she promised King Merry.

But just as the words left her mouth, something dreadful happened!

Right in front of the racing unicorns, a cluster of long green weeds broke

through the surface of the track. The
thick stalks immediately began to
grow, snaking out across the grass in all
directions. The nasty
plants slithered out
and tangled
themselves in
the legs of the
running
unicorns.
Four of the
runners got so
tripped up they
fell horn over hoof.

Littlehorn only escaped by
leaping high into the air as a stalk tried
to grab her tail.

"What on earth are those?" cried Ellie
as one of the weeds burst up through

the ground at Jasmine's feet. Ellie and Summer grabbed it and pulled as hard as they could, but the wriggling stem slipped out of their hands and kept on growing.

"It must be because of the Great Apple Tree!" Trixi cried. "With the caterpillars eating the fruit, the tree must be getting weaker. And since its magic is fading, the horrible weeds are coming back to Unicorn Valley! Quick, head for the hill!"

Everyone started running up the hill, but new vines began springing up all around them, and they had to dodge the stalks as they ran. The girls and unicorns managed to scramble to the top of the hill quickly, but King Merry lagged behind. He was out of breath, and Trixi had to help push him up the slope. They had almost reached the girls when a weed

curled around King Merry's foot and tripped him.

Ellie dashed down to help him, but one of the vines wound around her waist. As Summer and Jasmine watched in horror, the vicious vine started pulling her down the hill!

Storm Sprites!

"Get off my friend!" Jasmine shouted, hitting the stalk that was wound tightly around Ellie.

"Hold on!" Summer called, grabbing Ellie's hands.

Jasmine started tugging at the clinging vine. With both of them working together, the weed's grip soon started to loosen.

"It's working!" exclaimed Ellie. The vine finally lost its grip — and she, Jasmine, and Summer fell over in a big heap on the ground.

"Whew!" Ellie sighed. "That was close!" The girls struggled back to the top of the hill, where Trixi, King Merry, Littlehorn, and the other unicorns were standing.

"The weeds are growing out of control!" exclaimed Jasmine, pointing down the hill, where even more yucky plants were popping up.

"We'll have to cancel the Golden Games." King Merry frowned. "There's no way we can hold them here with all these weeds in the way. Trixi, could you send a glowworm announcement to warn everyone to stay away?"

Trixi tapped her ring, and it began to shine softly. A few moments later, lots of little lights appeared around them as hundreds of  glowworms woke up. The girls looked in amazement at the little lights that shone weakly in the daylight.

"There are glowworms across the kingdom," Trixi explained. "They'll pass our message on to everyone who sees them."

Trixi flew over to tell the glowworms the message, but Summer stopped her.

"Oh, please don't call off the games yet," she begged. "If you do, Queen Malice will get her way and all the unicorns will be miserable. Littlehorn and the others won't be able to get their golden horns, and King Merry won't get a new messenger. We have to fix this!"

"But what can we do?" Trixi cried anxiously. "Without the Great Apple Tree's magic, soon the valley will be completely ruined."

"Wait a minute," Ellie said. "We need to work out how we're going to break Queen Malice's thunderbolt. At King Merry's birthday party, we broke the spell by making sure everyone had fun. So if Queen Malice wants to ruin the Golden Games and the Great Race, then we have to make sure that they go ahead."

"But how?" Trixi asked. "We'll never clear all these weeds away in time, and we can't have the Great Race without a racetrack."

Summer smiled. "I have an idea! There's always a balance in nature, even if Queen Malice's magic is involved. We've got hungry caterpillars at the Great Apple Tree, and plants that won't stop growing at the racetrack. . . . I think we should take the caterpillars to the Golden Games!"

"The caterpillars won't enjoy the games!" King Merry spluttered. "They're very lazy and they don't like sports."

Ellie smiled as she realized what her friend had in mind. "Not to take part in the games!" She laughed. "If we bring the greedy caterpillars here, they'll eat up all the weeds!"

"They'll chomp the racetrack clean!" agreed Jasmine.

"And then the games can go on!" Summer said, beaming.

Trixi danced excitedly around on her leaf. "I really think it might

work, girls," she said. "Thank goodness you're here!"

"But how are we going to get back to the Great Apple Tree?" Jasmine asked, looking down at the weeds that were snaking all over the racetrack. "We're stranded!"

"I can take care of that!" Trixi said cheerfully. "Everyone hold hands — or hooves."

"I'll stay here, Trixi," King Merry announced. "Someone has to stay with the other unicorns and keep them calm."

"He doesn't like being magicked around," Trixi whispered to the girls. "It tangles up his beard and makes him dizzy!"

The girls giggled.

With Ellie, Summer, Jasmine, and Littlehorn all holding on to one another, Trixi cast a spell:

*"Help us get where we need to be:
Under the Great Apple Tree!"*

Ellie shut her eyes tightly, and when she opened them again they were all standing in the clearing by the tree. She hadn't felt a thing!

"The caterpillars are much bigger now," Summer said.

Trixi's magic spell was keeping the slime caterpillars from spreading, but they were growing quickly as they munched apple after apple and nibbled on the tree trunk.

One of the orchard-keeper unicorns sighed. "And the larger they get, the more they eat!"

"That's a good thing!" Jasmine grinned. "There are lots of horrible weeds growing

at the racetrack, and the caterpillars can help us by eating them all up! We just need to get them there. . . ." Suddenly, she spotted a large apple cart nearby with some fruit in it. "Aha!" she said. "That'll be perfect! If we load that cart full of the tastiest apples, the caterpillars are sure to jump in there, too."

Trixi released her holding spell, and Ellie and Summer set to work heaping armfuls of fruit into the cart. But the caterpillars paid no attention.

"If only we could get them to understand where we want them to go," said Summer thoughtfully.

"How could we do that?" asked Trixi.

Summer thought for a moment longer. "We need a trail of food to lead the caterpillars all the way to the cart."

"That's an excellent idea!" said Trixi, smiling. "I'll do it right away."

The little pixie tapped her ring. It glowed, then something green unfurled from it and fell to the ground. It was a crisp, fresh cabbage leaf.

More leaves appeared from her ring, and Trixi arranged them in a line, leading from the Great Apple Tree into the cart.

One of the caterpillars raised its head, sniffing the air. Then it licked its lips hungrily, crawled forward, and began to nibble at the leaf.

It wasn't long before excited caterpillars were following one another toward the cart. One by one they oozed closer and crawled up into the cart, leaving a slimy trail behind them.

Once all the caterpillars were gathered

up, the girls packed more apples and berries around them to make sure they had plenty to eat.

When everyone was ready, Trixi tapped her ring once more and the whole group was instantly transported back to the hill.

It was worse than they'd imagined. The racetrack was completely covered with horrible weeds, and King Merry was marooned at the top of the hill next to two sad-looking unicorns.

"We've brought the caterpillars from the Great Apple Tree," Ellie called up to him from the other side of the track. "They'll gobble these vines right up!"

By now, the caterpillars had finished eating the food in the cart. When the girls looked in, there was nothing to be seen except apple cores and enormous, sleepy caterpillars.

"What if they're too full to eat the weeds?" Summer asked anxiously.

But when the slimy creatures spotted the moving weeds, they woke up at once. They licked their lips and crawled toward them eagerly, making funny little gobbling sounds. They quickly began to chomp their way through the mass of twisty green stalks.

"Our plan is working!" Trixi said, clapping her hands delightedly and flying her leaf in a figure eight.

"Good job, Ellie, Summer, and Jasmine!" King Merry called, leading the unicorns down the hill.

"Soon the racetrack will be clear!" said Jasmine as the girls moved the rest of the caterpillars off the carts. "Nothing's going to stop us now!"

Ellie gasped and grabbed her friend's arm. "Uh-oh, something might," she said, pointing behind them. "Look back there."

The girls turned to look. Not far away, two horrid-looking creatures were flying toward the racetrack on top of thunderclouds. Their spiky fingers were outstretched and their dark eyes gleamed with nastiness.

"Queen Malice's Storm Sprites!" said
Summer.

The ugly creatures zoomed closer on
their thunderclouds. One of them blew
a raspberry at the girls.

"Give those caterpillars
to us!" the other
one shouted.
"We're going
to spread them
everywhere so
they eat every
single plant, tree,
and bush around.
Unicorn Valley will
become a wasteland, and there's nothing
you can do about it!"

A Slimy Surprise

"We can't let the Storm Sprites take the caterpillars!" Summer cried.

Just then, Jasmine noticed something by the entrance to the racetrack — a stand full of juicy-looking blue melons.

"Quick, help me grab some really big caterpillars," Jasmine said. "No time to explain — just trust me."

Ellie and Summer helped Jasmine
find three large caterpillars and carry
them toward the stall of melons. The
caterpillars were so fat now that each girl
could lift only one of them, and they were
very slimy!

"Whew!" puffed Ellie as she put her heavy caterpillar in place. "I get it, Jasmine. The caterpillars will make the ground slippery, and the Storm Sprites will fall over!"

"Brilliant idea," Trixi said as she flew overhead. "Those are sugar melons. They're so sweet and tasty the caterpillars won't be able to resist them!"

Sure enough, as soon as the caterpillars spotted the yummy-looking sugar melons, they crawled eagerly across the path to get to them, leaving three super-slippery trails behind them.

"Okay, you win," Jasmine called to the sprites. "We'll give you the caterpillars. Here, take these ones."

The sprites laughed nastily, then hopped off their thunderclouds and flew down to

the ground, narrowing their black eyes as if they were getting ready to spring.

"Whoa!" shouted the first sprite as he landed. "It's slippery!"

His foot shot out from underneath him and hit the other sprite on the ankle. The second sprite gave a wail, hopped on one leg, then stumbled his way across the road, waving his arms frantically.

The Storm Sprites had landed right in the slippery caterpillar goo!

Neither of them could find a firm place to stand. First they slid into each other, then they tried to grab each other. Finally they both fell down in a tangled heap among the sugar melons.

"You knocked me over, Slug-Breath," one of them shouted.

"No, you tripped me!" the other complained bitterly from underneath a squashed melon.

The girls stood beside the road, giggling at the sight of Queen Malice's henchmen lying surrounded by squashed melons and slime.

The unicorns laughed, too — all except Fleetfoot, Graycoat, and Sleekmane, who

were standing over the Storm Sprites, giving them very stern looks.

"You two are coming with us," Graycoat whinnied. "You can help us tidy up the orchard. That should keep you out of trouble until the Golden Games are over."

The unicorns marched the Storm Sprites off toward the orchard, with the sprites still bickering loudly and pushing and shoving each other.

"There won't *be* any games unless the caterpillars have cleared the track," Jasmine said anxiously. But when she looked at the racecourse, there wasn't a weed to be seen! The grass was visible again, and lying sleepily on it, looking fatter than ever, were the slime caterpillars! The one closest to Jasmine

was lying on its back, with its hundreds
of feet up in the air, snoring loudly.

Suddenly there was a whinny, and
Silvertail came racing up to them
from the direction of the Great Apple
Tree. "Queen Malice's thunderbolt has
broken!" she told them excitedly. "The
tree has already begun to repair itself!"

"We did it!" cried Jasmine.

"We will always be grateful for what you have done today," Silvertail said gravely. "But I am afraid there is still one problem."

The friends exchanged a look.

"The caterpillars!" they all said at once.

What were they going to do with the greedy creatures?

"We have to find somewhere else for them to live," said Trixi.

"Yes," Summer agreed. "We can't send the poor things back to Queen Malice."

But as they watched, the caterpillars started to wriggle. After a few moments, they had coated themselves in silk, which quickly hardened into solid cocoons.

"What's happening?" King Merry

asked. Silvertail knelt down and nudged
the nearest cocoon with her horn.

"I don't know," she said, "but at least
they won't need feeding for a while!"
Everyone helped move the cocoons
carefully into the cart, where they'd be

out of the way of the Golden Games. It
was a lot easier now that the caterpillars
weren't wiggling around!

"Just in time!" said Silvertail, smiling as
Jasmine put the last cocoon carefully into
the cart. "We're ready for the opening
ceremony. Summer, Ellie, and Jasmine,
you must stay and be our guests of
honor."

Silvertail led the girls to the best spot
on the hill, next to King Merry. Trixi
magicked up floating cushions for them
all, and they settled down as the young
unicorns made the final preparations for
the games.

Once everything was ready, King
Merry's cushion floated up above the
spectators, and he nervously read out
his speech.

"It is my address to honor you this year. . . ." he started to say, getting his words hopelessly jumbled up again.

Summer, Ellie, and Jasmine found it difficult not to giggle, but they didn't want to upset the kindly king. They did their best and managed to stay straight-faced until he had finished.

Then they forgot about laughing as the parade of competitors began. Lots of little unicorns strutted confidently around the track. They all had different ribbons, flowers, and grasses woven into their manes and tails.

The girls all cheered as Littlehorn cantered past proudly.

Finally the unicorns lined up in front of the audience and sang the Secret Kingdom's national song:

*"The Secret Kingdom is a
wonderful land
From frosty mountain to
glittery sand.
Every unicorn, imp, and gnome
Loves our beautiful magical home."*

After they'd sung all the verses, the stadium went quiet.

"Look!" Ellie cried, pointing at the sky. All the little unicorns had raised their heads, and pink and red sparkles were shooting from the tips of their horns like fireworks! The

sparkles swirled and twisted into huge
letters that twinkled brightly in the
evening sky.

"Thank you, Summer,
Ellie, and Jasmine,
for breaking Queen
Malice's spell!"

Summer read out loud.
"Wow!" whispered Jasmine.
Then the letters joined and changed,
coming together again to spell out:

Let the Golden
Games begin!

The Golden Games

The girls oohed and aahed in wonder
as they saw one amazing event after
another. Some of the graceful unicorns
took part in a jumping race, leaping
over hurdles made of shimmering magic.
Others jumped high in the air to catch
golden hoops on their horns. There was
so much going on that Ellie, Summer, and
Jasmine hardly knew where to look first!

The high point of the games was the Great Race. Summer, Ellie, and Jasmine held on to their cushions with excitement as Silvertail fired a burst of sparkles from her horn to start the race and the unicorns sped off.

"Come on, Littlehorn!" chanted the girls.

At first Littlehorn was in the lead! But a larger, red-dappled unicorn was running on the inside lane, and he was gradually overtaking her. . . .

Jasmine stood up and shouted encouragement while Ellie cheered and Summer crossed her fingers and pressed them against her cheeks.

Trixi was so excited she couldn't bear to look, so she hid behind her human friends. "Tell me when it's over!" she said.

Littlehorn put on a burst of speed, creeping closer and closer to the larger unicorn.

"You can do it, Littlehorn!" Jasmine yelled at the top of her lungs. Littlehorn lowered her horn determinedly and galloped as fast as she could. She caught up to the other unicorn — and won by a horn!

Trixi and the girls watched with pride as King Merry crowned Littlehorn with a wreath of glitterberries and officially named her as his new royal messenger.

Finally all the young unicorns climbed up to the top of the hill and were greeted by their family and friends. The celebrations were nearly over, and the girls knew it was almost time for them to go home. Only one last thing remained — to watch Littlehorn and the other young unicorns get their golden horns!

Silvertail whinnied and the unicorns all fell silent. "This is when we perform the coming-of-age ceremony," she said, "and when we honor those who help us."

Littlehorn suddenly looked very serious. She and the other young unicorns gathered in a circle facing inward and

slowly lowered their heads. As their horns touched, there was a tinkling sound, and the air above the circle started to glow. The girls gasped in wonder as the little unicorns' horns slowly changed from a sparkling silver to a glorious golden color. As soon as the change was complete there was a great roar of noise as all the unicorns neighed and stomped their hooves in celebration. Littlehorn grinned widely, going cross-eyed in her attempts to look at her newly golden horn.

The noise died down as Silvertail moved into the middle of the circle. She gave a long whinny, and all of the unicorns pointed their horns to one spot in the air. Bursts of sparkly magic streamed out of their horns, coming together to form

a glittery shape. Slowly the shape came into focus — it was a tiny silver unicorn horn! When it was complete, Silvertail whinnied again and the horn floated over to the girls.

"This is a gift to thank you for saving Unicorn Valley from Queen Malice's

meanness. Without you, our beautiful home would have been destroyed. We will always be grateful," said Silvertail, bowing to the girls. Behind her, the unicorns bowed their heads. Even Trixi, with a huge smile on her little face, dipped a little curtsy.

Summer realized all the unicorns were waiting for them to take the gift. She stepped forward nervously and carefully grasped the sparkling horn. It was no longer than her little finger, and seemed to weigh almost nothing. It was covered with a beautiful spiral pattern, just like Littlehorn's. Just then there was a gasp from the crowd. The girls turned and peered down at the apple carts. The caterpillar cocoons were moving and

shaking. All of a sudden, one of them popped open and a gorgeous butterfly with shimmering purple patterns on its wings flew up into the air! The cocoons were hatching! Soon, another butterfly appeared, and then another, until the air was filled with them, dancing and fluttering about on their new wings.

"They're beautiful!" Summer exclaimed.

"Who'd have thought those slimy caterpillars could become such gorgeous butterflies." Jasmine smiled.

"I hope they won't be quite as hungry now that they're grown-up," Ellie said.

Everyone admired the beautiful butterflies as they flitted and fluttered above, oohing and aahing at their dance in the sky.

After a few minutes, Silvertail hushed the crowd. "We will be silent for a moment," she said seriously. "Now, Summer, listen carefully."

Summer did so, wondering what was supposed to happen.

Then she gasped. Among the flapping of their wings, she could suddenly hear the butterflies calling out.

"Thank you!" they all cried. "We didn't mean to cause any trouble."

"I can understand the butterflies!" she said in amazement.

Ellie and Jasmine listened hard. "I can't hear anything," Ellie said.

"The silver horn gives you the ability to talk to and understand all animals," said Trixi, smiling.

Summer handed the horn to her friends so that they could hear the little voices.

Trixi tapped her ring and a sparkly spell in the shape of a butterfly appeared and flew away, leaving a glittery trail. "This will lead you to Flower Forest," she told the beautiful butterflies.

As the butterflies started to follow Trixi's spell to their new home,

Silvertail turned to the girls solemnly. "You are now honorary members of our unicorn family. You are Summer Kindhoof. You are Ellie Flamemane. And you are Jasmine Braveheart," she said as she gently touched each of the girls in turn with her horn. "Should you ever need us, we will be there to help you."

The girls looked at one another in amazement. "Thank you," Jasmine managed to say.

Smiling happily, the girls said good-bye to the unicorns. Trixi kissed each girl on the nose, then hovered above their heads and conjured up the magic whirlwind that would take them back home.

"See you soon!" was the last thing they heard as they were lifted higher and higher above beautiful Unicorn Valley.

Then, with a flash of light, they found themselves settling softly onto Ellie's rug.

Ordinary daylight filled the bedroom, and glinted off the Magic Box, which was sitting on the rug between them.

"Oh, wow," said Ellie, looking down at the little horn in her hand. "What an amazing adventure."

"I'm so glad we met the unicorns," said Summer.

"But it's a shame that time doesn't pass while we're in the Secret Kingdom," sighed Jasmine. "After all that, I'm hungrier than ever — and the cookies *still* aren't ready!"

Ellie and Summer laughed.

Suddenly the Magic Box began to glow, and its lid slowly opened. Ellie gently placed the silver horn into one of the

compartments inside. "I hope we can
go back to the Secret Kingdom soon,"
she said.

"You can count on that, Flamemane,"
said Jasmine with a chuckle. "We still
have to find four more of those nasty
thunderbolts. I wonder where we'll
go next. How about the Wandering

Waterfalls? Ooh, or the Mystic Meadows? King Merry said the pixies have toadstool fights there!"

"I'd love to see both of those places." Summer sighed. "But the important thing is to be there for Trixi and King Merry, and to save the kingdom from Queen Malice!"

"That's for certain," agreed Jasmine, grinning. "All right — race you to the cookies!"

Laughing, the three friends ran downstairs.

In the next Secret Kingdom
adventure, Ellie, Summer, and
Jasmine visit

Cloud Island!

Read on for a sneak peek. . . .

A Message from the
Secret Kingdom

"I wish we didn't have so much homework to do." Ellie Macdonald sighed as
she walked home from school with
her friends. "I've got to write a story for
English, and I don't know where to start!"

"Let's all do our homework together
at my house," suggested Jasmine Smith.
"We can put some music on and help
one another."

"Great idea," agreed Summer Hammond, linking arms with Jasmine and Ellie. "Even homework can be fun when you do it with friends."

"I wouldn't go that far." Ellie grinned, her green eyes twinkling. "But it's better than doing it on your own."

Laughing, they all made their way to Jasmine's house and hurried into the kitchen.

A big bag of chocolate cookies and a note were sitting on the kitchen table. Jasmine picked up the note and read it out loud:

"Hi, Jasmine,
I'm sure you've brought Ellie
and Summer back with you,
so share these with them! There's some
homemade lemonade in the fridge as well.

See you at five.
Mom."

"Your mom's so nice!" said Summer.

Jasmine smiled. "I wonder what made her think you'd be with me."

"Yeah, you would think we spent all our time together," joked Ellie.

Summer giggled. She, Jasmine, and Ellie all lived in a little town called Honeyvale and went to the same school. They had been best friends since they were little, and they went over to one another's houses so much that they all felt like home!

Jasmine opened the fridge and took out a big jug of lemonade while Summer grabbed three glasses and a plate.

"Now, let's deal with our homework," said Jasmine, putting everything on a tray and leading the way upstairs. "Then we can start having some real fun."

"Hey, you've got the Magic Box on your dressing table!" exclaimed Ellie as they all spilled into Jasmine's bedroom, which was quite small, but beautifully decorated. The walls were a gorgeous hot-pink color, and red floaty netting hung down over the bed.

"I didn't want to miss a message from the Secret Kingdom!" Jasmine said.

They all looked at the beautiful wooden box. It was covered with intricate carvings of fairies and unicorns and had a mirrored lid studded with green stones. It looked like a jewelry box, but it was *much* more than that.

"I slept with it under my pillow last time I was taking care of it!" Ellie laughed.

The girls had found the Magic Box at a school rummage sale, when it had mysteriously appeared in front of them. It belonged to King Merry, the ruler of the Secret Kingdom.

The Secret Kingdom was a magical world that no one knew existed — no one except Jasmine, Summer, and Ellie! It was a beautiful crescent moon–shaped island, where mermaids, unicorns, pixies, and elves all lived happily together.

But the kingdom was in terrible trouble. Queen Malice, the king's horrible sister, was so angry that the people of the Secret Kingdom had chosen King Merry to be their ruler instead of her that she had sent six horrible thunderbolts into the

kingdom to cause all kinds of trouble. Summer, Jasmine, and Ellie had already found two of the thunderbolts and broken their nasty spells.

"I wish we could go on another magical adventure." Ellie sighed.

"Me too," agreed Jasmine, taking her books out of her backpack and sprawling out on the carpet. She tucked her long dark hair behind her ears. "Come on, let's get this over with," she said, reaching for a chocolate cookie.

Ellie got her English book out and started chewing on her pencil. She was looking around the room, trying to come up with an idea for her story, when something caught her eye. "I don't think we'll be doing homework after all!" she cried in delight. "The Magic Box is glowing!"

The girls all jumped up to look. They crowded around the box, watching excitedly as, letter by letter, words started to form in the magic mirror.

"I wonder what mischief Queen Malice is up to now," said Jasmine, shuddering at the thought of the horrid queen and her wicked plans to make everyone in the kingdom as miserable as she was.

"We'll have to solve the riddle to find out," said Summer as she studied the words in the mirror. Then she slowly read them out loud:

"A thunderbolt there will be found
Way up high above the ground.
A white and fluffy floating land
Needs you all to lend a hand!"

Jasmine quickly wrote the riddle down before the words disappeared into the mirror. "What does it mean?" she asked.

Ellie looked puzzled. "A floating land — it must be an island."

"Let's check the map," said Jasmine. "We might be able to spot it."

As if it had heard them, the Magic Box opened up, revealing the six compartments inside. Only two of the spaces were filled, one by a map of the Secret Kingdom that King Merry had given them after their first visit, and the other by a little silver unicorn horn. It was small, but it had enormous power — whoever held it could talk to animals!

Summer took out the map carefully and spread it out gently on Jasmine's floor.

The three girls sat around it, their heads touching as they peered at it excitedly. There were a few small islands in Mermaid Reef, and a couple more off the shore of Glitter Beach. They all moved magically on the map as the aquamarine sea bobbed up and down, but none of them looked white or fluffy.

"It's not here!" Summer said anxiously.

"But it has to be!" cried Ellie. "We have to solve the riddle so we can get to the Secret Kingdom and find the thunderbolt before something horrible happens!"

Jasmine stood and started pacing up and down the middle of her room with a worried expression on her face.

"Let's read the riddle again," Summer suggested. "We have to be missing

something. 'A white and fluffy floating land.' Well, these islands aren't white or fluffy."

"'Way up high above the ground . . .'" Jasmine muttered to herself. Then she glanced down at the map and laughed. Summer and Ellie were still searching the bottom of the map, looking at every inch of sea. But Jasmine had realized something. "We shouldn't be looking in the sea!" she cried. "We should be looking in the sky!"

"Of course!" said Ellie with a grin. "What's white and fluffy and floats?"

"A cloud!" exclaimed Summer.

"And here's Cloud Island!" Ellie exclaimed, pointing to a puffy white cloud at the top of the map. "That must be it. Let's summon Trixi!"

The girls put their hands on the Magic Box, pressing their fingers against the green stones on its carved wooden lid.

"The answer is Cloud Island," Jasmine whispered.

Suddenly there was a flash of light, followed by a squeal. Trixibelle had appeared, but the little pixie was trapped among the netting over Jasmine's bed!

"Keep still!" Jasmine cried as the little pixie twisted around. She was trying to free herself, but was only getting more and more caught up.

"I'm trying!" Trixi cried, giving a yelp as she tumbled off her leaf.

Ellie, Jasmine, and Summer quickly climbed up onto Jasmine's bed to untangle Trixi from the mesh. Ellie's

nimble fingers carefully unwrapped the netting from Trixi's flower hat, while Jasmine and Summer helped Trixi pull her arms and legs free.

"There!" Ellie said as she untangled the last bit.

"Whew!" Trixi sighed, jumping back on her leaf and flying in a quick twirl before straightening out her skirt and the flower hat that covered her messy blond hair. "Hello, girls," she exclaimed, flying over to kiss them all on the tips of their noses. She landed on the edge of Jasmine's bedside table. "It's lovely to see you all again. Have you figured out where the next thunderbolt is?"

"We think it's somewhere called Cloud Island," Summer said.

Trixi nodded. "There's no time to waste! We need to go to the kingdom right away."

The girls all looked excitedly at one another. They were off on another magical adventure — this time to an island in the sky!

As the girls watched, Trixi tapped the Magic Box with her ring and chanted a spell:

*"The evil queen has trouble planned.
Brave helpers fly to save our land."*

Her words appeared on the mirrored lid and then soared toward the ceiling, separated into sparkles, and tumbled down again in a colorful burst, whizzing around the girls' heads until they formed

a whirlwind. The rushing air picked the girls up, and moments later Ellie, Summer, and Jasmine were dropped onto something springy. It was the softest landing ever!

Summer looked around in astonishment. It felt like she was on a huge bouncy bed, but all she could see around her was white. Hesitantly, she put out her hand to touch the fluffy stuff, and then grinned as she realized — she was standing on a cloud!

Read

Cloud Island

to find out what happens next!

In the next Secret Kingdom
adventure, Ellie, Summer, and
Jasmine visit

Mermaid Reef

Read on for a sneak peek. . . .

A Message at School

"Another thunderbolt is near,
Way down deep in water clear.
Look on the bed that's in the sea,
Where more than fish swim happily!"

Ellie slowly read out the rhyme. "What
do you think that means?"

Jasmine frowned. "Well, the bottom of
the sea is called the sea*bed* . . ."

Suddenly the Magic Box glowed again and the lid magically opened, revealing the six little wooden compartments inside. Three of the spaces were already filled with the wonderful gifts they'd been given by the people of the Secret Kingdom. There was a magical moving map that showed them all the places in the kingdom, a tiny silver unicorn horn that let them talk to animals, and a shimmering crystal that had the power to change the weather.

"Maybe the map will give us a clue," said Jasmine. She carefully took it out of the Magic Box and smoothed it out. It showed the whole of the Secret Kingdom spread out beneath them, as if the girls were looking down at it from high above.

"Look," Jasmine said, pointing to the aquamarine sea. Waves were gently spilling onto the shore, colorful fish were playing in the water, and a beautiful girl was sitting on a rock, combing her hair.

As Ellie, Summer, and Jasmine watched, the girl dived off the rock into the sparkling water. Jasmine gasped as she saw that, instead of legs, the girl had a glittering tail!

"Did you see that?" she cried to the others, who nodded excitedly. "She's a mermaid!"

Summer's eyes widened. "That must be it! 'More than fish swim happily' — we must be going to help mermaids!"

They leaned over the map again and watched the mermaid as she swam

down to where an underwater town was marked. Ellie held the map up and looked at the place name. "'Mermaid Reef,'" she read. "That must be where we're going."

Jasmine and Summer agreed, and the three friends quickly placed their fingertips on the jewels on the Magic Box.

Summer smiled at the others and said the answer to the riddle out loud: "Mermaid Reef."

The green jewels sparkled and a glittering light beamed out from the mirror, throwing dancing patterns onto the walls. Then there was a golden flash and Trixi appeared, twirling in midair like a ballerina! Her blond hair was even messier than usual, but she had a huge grin and her blue eyes twinkled happily as she balanced on her leaf.

"Hi, Trixi," Ellie cried in delight as the pixie hovered gracefully just in front of the girls.

"Hello," Trixi said, smiling. "Goodness, where are we?"

"We're at school!" Jasmine told her.

"Oh," Trixi said as she flew around the toilet stall on her little leaf. "This isn't at all what I thought an Other Realm school would look like. Where do you all sit?"

The girls giggled. "This isn't a classroom," Summer explained. "It's just the bathroom. We had to make sure no one would see us being swept off to the Secret Kingdom."

"Of course, silly me." Trixi smiled, but then her face took on a worried expression. "Do you know where Queen Malice's next thunderbolt is?"

"We think so," Ellie told her. "It seems to be somewhere called Mermaid Reef."

"Then we must go at once!" Trixi exclaimed. "The mermaids will need our help."

"We *are* going to meet mermaids!" Summer squealed as she jumped up and down in excitement.

Trixi giggled, then tapped her ring and chanted:

"The evil queen has trouble planned.
Brave helpers fly to save our land!"

As she spoke those words, a magical whirlwind surrounded the girls, twisting and turning around them.

"Wheeee!" Summer shouted as the wind

whipped her long blond hair around her face. "We're off on another adventure!"

Seconds later, the whirlwind set them down on a smooth green rock in the middle of the aquamarine sea. The girls were all delighted to be wearing their sparkly tiaras once again, although they were still in their school uniforms!

Jasmine looked around in surprise. "I thought we were going underwater?" she asked Trixi, a confused look on her face.

"We are!" Trixi said with a smile as she landed on the rock beside them, rolled up her flying leaf, and tucked it under her flower hat.

Suddenly the ground beneath them started to shake.

"What's going on?" Ellie cried.

The girls watched nervously as the water started to churn in front of them, foaming and frothing as something large and dark rose up out of the depths.

Suddenly a huge green head appeared out of the water. Ellie and Jasmine gasped in fear and squeezed their eyes shut, but Summer broke out in a grin. "Look!" she cried, pointing at the animal's face. The creature blinked at them with sparkling brown eyes and gave them a lazy smile. "This isn't a rock we're standing on — it's the back of a gigantic sea turtle!"

"A lift from a friendly turtle is the only way to get to Mermaid Reef!" Trixi said. The little pixie tapped her ring and a stream of purple bubbles shot out of it, flying all around the girls in a

whirlwind, then bursting over their heads and showering them with purple glitter.

"Hold on tight!" Trixi called, pointing to the top of the turtle's shell, where there was a ridge they could grab on to. "One . . . two . . ."

"Trixi, wait!" Jasmine cried. "We can't breathe underwater!"

But it was too late.

"Three!" Trixi called, tapping her ring once more, and with a great lurch the huge turtle dived deep into the sea . . .

Read

Mermaid Reef

to find out what
happens next!

Be in on the secret.
Collect them all!

Enjoy six sparkling adventures.
www.secretkingdombooks.com